Praise for the
13 Reasons
for Murder
Series

"…hard to put down and am keen to read the next in the series."—Reader's Favorite 5-Star

"Full of sass, good friends, and a bit of blood, this novel was a joy to read."—Julie E.

"…suspenseful, addictive…hope there are more books with this character."—BookBub Review

"I look forward to…learning more about Britney."—Studiohnh.com Review

"…oddly addictive…cannot wait for the next book…"—Amazon.ca Review

"…flows at a quick pace and leaves you wanting more…"—Goodreads Review

"The plot is fresh and unique, a nice change to read something a little different…"—Reader's Favorite 4-Star

"…well written and kept me on the edge of my seat…"—Heather W.

13 Reasons for Murder: Philistines

(A Britney Cage Serial Killer Novel, 13 Reasons for Murder #3)

Amanda Byrd

Blacksheep Press, LLC

For the fans. Your support and belief in me have made my author's journey the most rewarding one of my life.

About the
Author

Amanda Byrd is obsessed with fictional serial killers. From Patrick Bateman to Dr. Hannibal Lecter to Dexter Morgan and every butcher in between, Amanda loves figuring out what drives fiction's deadliest monsters. When she's not busy writing, Amanda can be found reading, playing video games, or watching shows and movies like Mindhunter, Hannibal, and Dexter. She lives in Florida with her bloodthirsty, flesh-eating cat . And her husband.

Follow Amanda online: www.amandabyrd.net
Sign up for my Deadly Insiders Club and get a free story

Follow Amanda online:
Facebook: Author Amanda Byrd
Instagram: amanda_byrd_author
Goodreads: Amanda Byrd
Bookbub: Amanda Byrd

Contents

One

THE GIRLS LOOKED AT me funny. Again. I guess I made a noise or something because they all started asking me if I was okay. I was, sort of.

I'd already run into those Asian bitches in the bathroom, and now they were being even bigger bitches in the room next door. I understood cultural pride, but that didn't mean you could be rude in the adopted culture you're now living in. Let me clarify—or try to: If I'm living in your culture, know what's expected and considered rude, and am rude anyway, that would upset people. That's what these two sisters were doing now and had done in the bathroom. I swore I heard one of them talk shit about Americans.

We may not be the best people on the face of the planet, but we're not the worst either. And these two ungrateful bitches—badmouthing the country that had taken them in—well, these two had made my list. Had shot to the top of it, in fact, and I was ready to kill already.

All that training and hard work in China and for what? Me to have yet another reason to kill someone? No, two someones, actually, but I wondered if all that time I spent in China trying to center myself could be undone, just like that, by a flash of anger. It didn't matter; I felt the urge. I'd get it done somehow, but I was more worried about the patience part. I'd need to remember my lessons from the monastery.

Three months with monks and even more time here trying to become a more patient person. Now it would be put to the test. I'd need to make doubly sure I planned this out completely, just to ensure I'd knocked off any mental rust that might have accumulated during my time of isolation, study, and introspection.

Sure, I could knock these two off now and maybe *not* draw suspicion, but it had only been a few months, and I was well aware of patterns. You know, those patterns that got killers caught if the cops suspected anything. I wasn't going to leave a trace. I brought my focus back to dinner, where the girls were sipping drinks and laughing. They'd gone back to their chatter once I'd told them I was fine.

I joined in the conversation. We talked about everything: my trip to Heather's practice, Danielle's promotion, and Sarah's and Kristen's kids and crazy lives.

Eventually, it got getting late, and we were running out of wine. Julie looked at her watch, and shock crossed her face. "I told Cody I wouldn't be out late." She looked at me, smirking.

"Oh, because *I'm* the bad influence!"

A chorus of yeses followed, and we all burst into fits of laughter. "Okay, you got me," I said. "I suppose that means we're not going back to my place for a few more bottles?"

The girls laughed, and we made actual plans to have another sleepover night at my place. See, my house was the getaway house. I was rarely home, and if one of the girls wanted to get out of theirs for a few days, mine served as Airbnb. It was just something that was understood. I'm single, no roommate except Minion…It made sense. And no one had to spend any extra money unless they really wanted to get out of state.

We paid our checks and left together. Apparently, we'd all valeted our cars, and the poor valet guy was suddenly barraged with pickup tickets from six women, two of whom could have been cougars if they really wanted.

Sarah's minivan was first, then Heather's SUV. The rest came along, and the girls left. Mine was saved for last. I guess the valet wanted me to be his cougar for the night because when I tipped him, he mentioned what time he got off, in particular tones that screamed he wanted to have sex. I gave him my number. Good sex was hard to find, and I wasn't opposed to testing out a younger model. I got in my Jeep and drove home, giggling most of the way.

It was already ten, and I wanted nothing more than to shower and go to sleep. I walked in and set my shoes on the stand I kept near the door. Minion screamed at me from somewhere, my bedroom maybe, and ran right to the spot I place her bowl during feeding time. I'd beaten her to the punch, and she was happy to have food, though I'm sure she enjoyed judging me too.

I'd started up the stairs when my phone rang. I fished it out of my purse to see a number I didn't recognize and answered anyway. It was the valet. We chatted a bit, and I texted him my address. I continued upstairs, this time with a much different mindset.

I couldn't decide if I should go for the lingerie or pajamas, though I ultimately went full-on cougar with the lingerie. If the kid didn't appreciate it, this would never happen again, and depending how the ride was, I might be okay with that. I'd just covered myself with a robe when he rang the bell. I took my time walking down to answer. When I did, and he walked in, I let my robe slip off as I led him upstairs. He must've tripped over either his jaw or the stair before he made it up to grab my hand and be led wherever I wanted to take him.

In the dim light just before sunrise, I woke and rolled over, gazing at the boy. He was twenty-one to my almost thirty. It was all okay, and as I looked over his sleeping face, a smile formed and he opened his eyes. He kissed me, and we had another delightful romp. Talk about morning glory.

When we were finished, I went to shower, casually picking my lingerie up on my way into the bathroom. I intended to wash it by hand, but the valet—I think his name was Devin?—joined me. He had class in an hour, and it was bad enough he still had last night's clothes. I laughed and kissed him on the cheek as I stepped out, wrapping a towel around myself.

"You should learn to keep extra clean clothes in your car."

"Oh?" He turned the shower off and pulled a towel to his face.

"You have much to learn," I smirked. In my head, I heard Yoda's voice and tried not to cry laughing. I brushed my teeth and finished getting ready. At some point in the middle, Devin said "Bye" and rushed out the door.

I headed down the stairs to make some coffee and watch the morning news. I still didn't have to be back at the office until Monday, but I was so bored I thought I might actually need a padded room just for fun. Or maybe an adult bouncy house. I needed something to focus on, and my killer brain immediately turned to the Asian sisters. The thought of killing two people and the challenges that posed making my heart skip a beat. I was excited and nervous and every other mixed emotion I could feel. This would be my first time killing two people so close together. I'd already had a vague idea how I wanted them to die; this time the kill spot and body dump eluded me. I took a deep breath. It was only the beginning and I needed to keep that foremost in my mind. I was a little out of practice after three months in Asia, but I could feel the machinery in my serial-killer mind slowly kicking into place.

The coffee was done making its gurgling noises, so I got up and poured myself a cup, adding four ice cubes. I blew on it and sipped as I walked back to the couch. It was too early in the morning to be this bored. I really needed something to do. The problem was that the house was already spotless, the laundry already finished. I couldn't even wash the Jeep because I had it detailed while I was gone. I grunted and continued to drink my coffee.

My phone chimed from upstairs. I set the mug on the coffee table and went to get it. It couldn't have been terribly important considering it was just a text. When I picked it up from its stand, I saw that it was Devin. He apologized for running out on me.

You didn't run out on me, I texted back with a smiley face.

Okay. I just wanted you to know I'm still thinking about last night and this morning, and I want it to happen again…

I was officially a cougar. And highly amused by this thought.

Well, when do you want to come back?

Now but I have class 'til three.

Go home after class, do what you have to do, then text me when you're on your way back.

I could handle this so long as he didn't get attached. That was my one peeve, and I made sure he knew it last night. I'd always remind anyone of the boundaries, and of the consequences of crossing them, using John Sweet as the perfect example. It didn't help the matter of boundary breaking that he broke into my house and poked through it and I walked in on him. That resulted in him being shot in the foot. He also lost his job as a cop. Not my problem he couldn't get it out of his head that I was a killer and murdered Alex Charles almost a year ago.

Wow, had it been that long already? I looked at the calendar. It really was almost a full year. I guess the saying about time flying when you were having fun was true…to a degree. I had patience issues last year, and I still kind of did. I wasn't rushing out for my next kill. Not now. That would definitely make me a suspect on some level. I'd only been back a few weeks and had left a few weeks after I killed Brody.

Of course, the cops didn't know I killed Brody either. I was never even questioned. His friends had no ideas, to no one's surprise. The hospital he worked for gave the names of a few coworkers, though. Apparently, there were altercations and words had. Also to no one's surprise. Brody was an all-around douche, and everyone knew it.

These Asian girls, though, were loved by the whole party that was with them, which likely meant they had an entire social network here in the bay area. I wondered how loved and how missed they'd be when they went missing. Not to sound obnoxious, but if they were as loved as me, someone would notice in less than twenty-four hours.

The stalk would feel like an endless pursuit, but the euphoria of the dual kill I could only imagine.

Two

I WENT BACK TO The Pub to see if anyone knew who they were or could give me any information on them. It wasn't like they told me their names when they were talking shit in the bathroom. The manager was able to pull the reservations from that night, and the sisters were on it. He happily gave me their names and address. That may have had something to do with how often my friends and I were there and how much we spent. I hugged and kissed him on the cheek before leaving. We even agreed to have lunch next week.

I hopped in my Jeep, listening to Marilyn Manson, Black Veil Brides, Fozzy, and Starset on the way home. I loved a wide variety of music, and my friends always make fun of me. The most at karaoke. I knew damn near every song from the '90s until now, that garbage that passes for rap/R&B/hip-hop these days excluded. I just loved music and appreciated the good stuff, which was most of it. I was singing as I backed in my driveway and got out of my Jeep.

I'm unstable, I'm not a show horseI can't be bridled, of courseI'm outstanding, I'm unregrettedI got tattooed in reverse
Woah, in reverse

I danced as I walked to the front door, unlocked it, walked into the house. I stopped singing and hummed my way to the kitchen table and my laptop. I grinned as I lifted the screen and pressed the power button. It booted quickly, asking for my password and opening the browser faster than usual. I'd done a thorough backup and cleaning of the hard drive before I went to China. I took it with me and wasn't about to be caught with anything they deemed inappropriate. I'd eventually get a solid-state-drive laptop, but I didn't feel like spending the money right now. It wasn't a matter of couldn't afford to; it was a matter of feeling like it—and I didn't. Then again, I never felt like paying bills.

I typed their names into the basic search engine first. All the usual pay background check sites listed on the first page. The good stuff was typically buried a few pages back. I went to the fifth page to start. Twenty minutes later, there wasn't much to show except a waste of time. No big deal. I had the software installed and registered to a friend who ran a background investigation company. I had to enter each sister separately. Nothing much there, only when they emigrated here as infants.

I did obtain the standard information of birthdates, home address, and phone numbers. Nothing I physically wrote down but committed to memory and saved on an encrypted micro-SD card. I know the technology could get me caught as easily as having used a pen, but this particular tech would be a little harder to get through. I used military-grade encryption. Having friends in high places helped. Still, having friends at places like SOCOM—Special Operations Command for the US Military—and not the city police department was odd. I'd never get used to it.

The sisters, Jimin and Suk McLaughlin, were both in their twenties, Suk being the elder. According to their DMV photos, Jimin was the shorter of the two at five-foot-one. Suk was five-foot-two. The major difference between the two, aside from Suk looking much older, was Suk's hair—she had red highlights. Jimin had nothing done to her hair, keeping it black. Suk looked like she was ten years older, at least. She must've had it rougher than Jimin. Not that looks mattered much beyond my need to distinguish them from each other.

I stopped a minute to think about this. They had a lot of friends and people who cared about them. This would be more of a challenge than I originally thought. I mean, to kill two instead of my usual one was challenge enough. Now I had to come up with something plausible for their family and friends to believe about their disappearance. Or did I? Was it worth all the trouble to go through? I'd much rather smash their phones before the kidnapping part. At the very least, make sure the phones were left at their shared apartment. Maybe I could work on their brakes so they'd conveniently have an "accident" in rush-hour traffic. Nah, too unpredictable.

I still had ketamine left from killing Brody, and these two might need about 1 cc each; they were smaller than me. I also had plenty of needles left. So there was that. I'd knock them out and take them. I needed to decide if I was going to take them separately or together, and I needed to plan out the kills and the disposal. I had time. It would come to me. The most important part was really the stalk. That had to be perfectly executed or I was fucked in so many ways.

Minion headbutted my foot, pulling me from my contemplations. She screamed at me with her pathetic and adorable meow. I couldn't bend down to pet her or I'd fall off the chair—they were the higher chairs, and the table was one they call a "high top." I shifted the chair and stood, then bent down to pick her up. We nuzzled a bit, and I set her back down, yawning. I needed some caffeine.

After getting the coffee going, I went back to my laptop and research. I opened my database to check if both women, or even just one, may have come through my office at some point. As luck would have it, they both had. I placed them at the accounting firm they were picked up by. I was sure they still worked there—they were pretty loyal, according to their personnel files. In those notes it stated they felt bad for leaving me but needed the permanent work. Ironic, wasn't it, that I was about to murder the kind of people I'd I opened Passing Through to help in the first place?

The coffee pot sang, and I paused my search to pour myself a cup. I wasn't sure I'd get used to this new coffee maker with all its beeps and singing. Why did electronics have to sing? I poured some peppermint mocha creamer in the cup and went back to work.

There wasn't much else I could do right then except look up their address listed with the DMV. Their licenses were newer than my records, so I chose to trust that. I almost spit out my coffee when I looked back at their licenses. They lived in the same apartments I used to. It was as though the universe was smiling on me.

Lakes of Northdale apartments were basically all the same layout, with few exceptions. The only issue I'd have was finding which building they were in. Not that I'd really call that an issue. No one ever noticed anything going on outside their own lives there. No one bothered to call in suspicious vehicles or people, only parties during the week. That was one of a short list of things I missed about living there. Not that I'd sell my house and go back.

Plus, a new management company took over and I wasn't hearing great things about them. A friend had driven by there a few weeks ago and called to tell me how rundown the complex was looking. For what they charged in rent, there was no reason for it to look that way. Now I had an opportunity to see it for myself.

The sun had already gone down for the day. I knew it wouldn't matter if I went tonight or during the day. Tomorrow was out. I had a lot of work to do around the house. Mainly just going through things to donate or trash. I felt cluttered, and it gave me agita. For tonight, I'd hang out and mentally plan. Maybe I'd even start thinking about the kill and dump. I knew I wanted both women to die the same way, watching each other suffer a slow death. The *how* eluded me for the moment, but I'd get it right. I always seemed to. It was a culmination of planning and the universe guiding me, or that's what I believed.

I washed and dried my coffee mug, then set it next to the coffee maker. When I put the creamer back in the refrigerator, I looked to see what I could eat for dinner. There were some peppers and sausage. Perfect. It was quick and easy to cook, which helped considerably. For as much as I put into my company and work, I'd say I was equally lazy sometimes when it came to putting in time for me. As far as I was concerned, it's allowed. And my concern is all that matters.

I sat on the couch and ate at the coffee table, half paying attention to the local news. All I cared about was the weather forecast. And even that was questionable sometimes. Mostly in the summer. Or in March. March was usually when summer weather started. June started hurricane season. Florida was, literally, a hot, wet mess, what could I say. That larger environment chaos was probably part of why I chose to live in south Tampa. I could jog in the early morning, or when I got home from work, and not be overwhelmed by the oppressive humidity.

My phone went off. I looked to see it was Devin. I smiled and responded with an invitation.

Three

Devin showed up not even twenty minutes later. I opened the door, and he stepped in, kissing me as I backed up to close and lock the door. It was like one of those cheesy rom-coms where they make out and go up to the bedroom and rip each other's clothes off. Except we weren't in love with each other, and this was real life.

He knew how to make me feel good. That surprised me because of his age, but who was I to judge? I definitely wasn't going to ask where his experience came from. I didn't care. I only cared about STDs, but he'd already told me he was clean. So was I. Then the sparks of pure pleasure made every nerve ending in my body explode. Not once, but twice before we fell asleep.

When we woke up, we went at it again. I couldn't believe how insatiable I'd become but I didn't wonder. I knew how I'd been in the past, and Devin really turned me on. When we finished, I took a shower and went to make breakfast while Devin took his shower. I started the coffee, fried up some eggs and bacon, toasted the remaining bread in the house. Devin came down pulling a shirt down over his six-pack, with wet hair, and smiled at me. I wanted him again, but he had to go to work. What a shame.

We ate breakfast and talked about our plans for the day. His, of course, consisted of working and a few papers he had to write for school. Mine should have been the start of stalking, but it hit me that I wasn't prepared to do so yet. I still needed to get my kill supplies restocked. The more I killed, the more I saw that having a full kill kit at all times was better planning and more efficient. Today would be a shopping day. One I couldn't tell Devin about, so I told him I had no plans.

I cleaned off the table and put all the dirty dishes in the dishwasher as we finished. Devin left, stopping himself short of kissing me goodbye. I was grateful for that. We get along, sure, but I don't want emotional attachment. I've got enough of that with Minion.

I called her name since she hadn't come looking for food when I was cooking. She came bounding into the kitchen like a tiny bull, being her dramatic little self. I hit start on the dishwasher and picked her up. She was less than thrilled, so I set her down and fed her. That made her happy.

I went back upstairs to see what I had left in the safe. The bag I'd packed for my last kill was in there, so I went through that first. By the time I was done going through everything, it looked like I needed another bucket, some six-millimeter plastic, and duct tape. Always with the duct tape. I figured I'd grab the needed bucket anyway in case I decided I actually wanted to use it somehow. Buckets were always good to have.

I got out some clothes that made it look like I was ready for a home improvement weekend and left. I knew better than to go to the same store I always went to, so I drove almost thirty minutes away. I purposely chose the locations in the seedier parts so I wouldn't look obvious or cause loss prevention to watch me, even from a recording days later. And I always played dumb if an employee approached me, saying something like I was helping a friend and this was what they asked me to get. That usually got them to walk away.

I'd picked up everything I came in for, paid, and left. By the time I got home, the sun should've been high, but it was shrouded by dark gray clouds. It smelled like rain was coming. I smiled and parked my Jeep in the garage, bringing everything I'd just bought to the safe. I locked it back up after repacking the bag and setting it inside the bucket for easier carrying.

I pulled my phone out of my pocket on the way back down-stairs, checking the forecast because I wanted to sit on the patio and watch the rain. The news said I had an hour or so until that happened. Then I heard the boom of thunder, and the sky opened up—so much for the accuracy of local news. Today was moving in my favor. I decided to cut up some smoked Gouda for a snack and ate it on the patio. Minion came to sit on my lap until a crack of lightning made her scurry inside. It was so close I heard a transformer blow. Luckily, my power wasn't affected.

Still, it hit a little too close, and the hair on my arms stood up. So did I. And walked inside, closing and locking the door behind me. I set my empty plate in the sink and sat on the couch, hitting the Netflix button on the remote. I flipped through my list until I found something I could nap to and laid my head on a pillow. Minion curled up with me, and we fell asleep in minutes as the rain pounded harder.

I woke to darkness, which didn't help much considering it got dark around dinner anyway. Minion glared at me as I shifted and sat up. I took my phone from the table and tapped the screen. It lit up, too bright, reading 5:16 p.m. It felt so much later. I walked to the kitchen to see what I had that I could make for dinner. There wasn't much left in the fridge, but there was a box of pasta, milk, some smoked Gouda, and other things I needed to make mac 'n' cheese. The meal left me full and guilty. I hadn't jogged today, but with as much pasta as I just ate, I swore I'd jog double tomorrow. I wrote myself a note to order groceries too.

I had no plans, and it was still pouring. I didn't want to fall asleep for another few hours so the pasta could digest a bit. I still needed a kill, so I put on some horror movies, looking for ideas. I started with the original *Pet Sematary*. At the end of that one, Gage…I'm not giving spoilers. I saw the remake too. I didn't hate it, but I didn't love it either. Then I watched *Touristas*, followed by the *Hannibal* TV show. I dissected assaults and deaths until I put one together for myself to complete. I'd use it on both sisters. I started to contemplate body dumps but came up empty. Maybe my brain was on overload?

I went back to *Hannibal* and finished season two before going up to bed. It was I-don't-know o'clock, and my eyelids were heavy. Once upstairs and in bed, I turned on my white noise app, put a sleep mask on, and curled up with Minion. I passed out to the sounds of static and unrelenting Florida rain.

Four

GOING FOR MY JOG was absolute hell. It was steamy and oppressive; I was sure I could've cut the air with a chainsaw if I'd tried. My pace was off, and the whole time I was outside was pure misery. Maybe I was having a hard time because I'd taken a day off.

When I got back into my air-conditioned house, I set the thermostat to sixty-five and let it work before attempting to take a shower. The last thing I wanted was sweating so bad I needed another shower after my shower.

I paced the house in the cool air for ten minutes before going to shower and change. Legitimately paced. I couldn't think of anything else to do. Coffee could wait, and I was too grumpy to want any. That bitter nectar of life I loved so much, and I didn't want any. There was something wrong, and that was how gross I felt in my own skin. Imagine you were dripping sweat. It was cold but also warm and sticky. And your hair was matted to your head. And your skin crawled like you were covered in a thousand spiders. And that was the easy way of describing the way I felt.

After my shower, I felt a lot better, and thankfully didn't sweat when I got out. Instead, I suffered severe goosebumps. I'm pretty sure I felt my leg hair even though I had just shaved. It was still preferable to the sweat. I dressed and reset the temperature to seventy-eight. That was the comfortable spot. My house got some natural light, though nothing major to make the air kick on during the day this early in the year. March, however, was a whole different ballgame.

The past few years, summer basically started mid-March and didn't end until December, if we were lucky. Climate change sure felt real, especially in the actual summer, when it felt like living on the sun. But I live where everyone vacations. It was insanity. I'd almost go so far as to say I was insane for staying here, but that would be inaccurate. I liked it here and had a lot going for me that I wasn't willing to give up just yet.

I'd been thinking a lot lately about my second office and if I wanted to move to another state—one with seasons—and open an office there. I wasn't miserable here and business was good. I had no real reason to go anywhere. This was one of those times I knew I needed more than one sounding board. So, I called Joe and got his voicemail, and I left a message. Then I sent a message in the group text with the girls asking them if they wanted to have a girls' night at my house next weekend.

When my phone dinged, I got excited, hoping it was Joe. He was always good for bouncing business ideas off of. He was good for everything, really. The man was a huge part of my success with Passing Through and like a second father to me. Or maybe it was one of the girls responding. It was neither.

What are your plans today? Devin asked.

Are you off?

I am, he responded with a winking face.

Well, I could shift some things and fit you in…

I'd really enjoy that

See you in an hour

I enjoyed this guy and our texts that were on the borderline of outright dirty. Keeping him at a distance was getting more difficult. The sex was too much fun and gratifying. We even talked like friends. Foremost in my mind, however, was not having to live a larger double life than I already did. Not getting caught was hard enough, and the first rule of being a serial killer was, duh, don't get caught. Having a significant other made it easier to do just that: get caught.

Still, my carnal urges won over, and while I waited for Devin to arrive, I made coffee and got laundry started. By the time the dryer sang its tune, Devin was knocking on the front door. I'd knocked back two cups of coffee and was a little caffeine high and jittery. I figured it would make for interesting sex. I wasn't used to caffeine jitters.

I let him in, and he winked then took off up the stairs. I laughed, closing and locking the door before following him.

He was down to his underwear, posing on his side on my bed. I laughed again, jumping on the bed right in front of him. The next hour was blissful as we tried to exhaust each other.

I heard my phone ringing and didn't care. I was too comfortable with my head on Devin's chest, his hands running through my hair. This was getting dangerously close to becoming something more. I kissed his chest and sat up, facing him.

"Devin," I hesitated, "this is getting too close—"

"To being a relationship," he said, cutting me off.

I shook my head. "Yes. Maybe we should cut back on seeing each other." I hated the words I was speaking. but there was no other option. I didn't want to see the kid get caught up in my hobby, which was what would happen if we kept seeing each other like this.

That told me I cared about him more than I was willing to admit, even to myself. Or maybe I just wanted him around a lot. Maybe it was just the sex with a hot younger guy. Regardless, I couldn't have it. My life wasn't fiction, and I wasn't about to risk everything over the possibility of that "forbidden" lust.

The fewer people who knew, or even suspected me, the better.

Devin was visibly bothered, but he agreed. I couldn't blame him. I wouldn't want to stop screwing me, either.

He got out of bed on the other side and put his clothes back on, and I stood and put a robe on. He walked around the bed, kissed me on the cheek, and said, "Call me whenever you want me. I'll be here," and left. He almost looked back but stopped himself. I just stood there like an idiot, watching him go. After he closed the door, I went down to lock it and then to take a shower.

I stood under the hot water until it went lukewarm, and then I finished up. I was so stuck on the fact that I'd started to care for Devin, it was all I could think about. I hated that I felt for him as much as I hated asking him to leave. It was so unfair. To be clear, I was not saying I wanted a relationship; it was never in my plans. It still wasn't. I couldn't think about how I'd be endangering someone else while out one night killing someone. I knew Minion would be taken care of if something happened to me. Julie would take her in, and she'd beat up on Julie's dog, Applesauce.

Turning the shower off, I was still lost in my own thoughts and anger when my phone went off again. I let out a groan and dried off, putting my pajamas on and going downstairs to see who wanted what. One was a text from Joe asking me over for brunch in the morning, and the other was Danielle responding to my group text. Whether next weekend would be just she and I remained to be determined—she was the only one to answer so far.

Phone in hand, I went back upstairs, calling Minion as I trudged. She came, tearing ass and trying to trip me. I sat on the bed, staring at the wall. Minion nudged my elbow and screamed at me, pulling me from the darkness that is my mind. I smiled and petted her before climbing under the blanket. She nuzzled under and into her spot in my hair. As much as I wanted to, I didn't fall asleep for another few hours.

Five

Monday morning, and I was on my way to Osten's house for brunch. It was weird not going into the office on time, considering I'd only been back a short time. I didn't have a whole lot of work to do, but it *was* my company. I didn't want to start research on a new office without bouncing things off Joe first, anyway. And I still wasn't sure if I was ready to open a second one. How could I justify it when we had so much downtime?

I pulled up to the gate at the end of his driveway and entered the code. The ornately crafted metal slid open, and I drove through as soon as the opening was large enough. The driveway itself was natural stone and fired clay designed in a giant U shape, with the house sprawling at the bottom of the U. I pulled up in front of Osten's garage and shut my Jeep off before jumping down out of the driver's seat. As I walked away, locking and arming it, I heard Osten's voice from the front door.

"Get over here and give this old man a hug," he boomed.

I picked up my pace, wrapping him as tight as I could. He bear-hugged me back. It was good to see him again. I hated long periods between seeing each other, but we were both busy. Joe less so after suffering a heart attack. He had peo-ple he trusted running the day-to-day of his office and only worked eight-hour days now. At the time of his heart attack, he was working fourteen-hour days and eating a high-cholesterol diet. Typical doctor.

Not that I was one to talk about that—I'd eat anything, but I also jogged almost every day.

Joe put an arm around my shoulders, and we walked into the kitchen. The spread was, as usual, incredible. Bagels, lox, cream cheese in four flavors, whitefish salad, eggs, bacon…everything I grew up eating to break the fast at Yom Kippur. I *still* didn't know where to find good whitefish salad in Southwest Florida, yet here it was on Osten's kitchen table. I drooled just seeing it all.

Osten motioned for me to sit down at one of the chairs. There was already coffee and orange juice waiting. I sat, waiting for him to sit too. The table was large enough for six people, me sitting in a chair toward one end. I expected Joe to sit in the end seat diagonal to me. He did. Then we started putting food on our plates and catching up about life in general.

"You said you wanted to bounce around new office ideas?"

I swallowed. "I did. I'm not sure I have enough work to justify the overhead yet. Basically, the same concern as last year."

"Well, you do have work toward the upper end of the county, and some in Pasco," he noted as he sipped his coffee.

"I do, but…I'll have to talk to the accountant and look at the books myself. I just feel like the slow months are so slow, I'll lose people because of it."

"We all lose employees, Brit. You can't let that stop you from growing."

He was right. My fears aside, I did want to grow—professionally and personally. This was more of a personal fear of being left that was somehow spilling over into my work. I'd always had it, and it was unjustified. No one who meant the world to me had left me of their own accord—I killed her. She was the only one I loved and killed. My family mess was just that and typical. We grew apart like a failed marriage that wasn't cared for.

But I needed, for once, to focus. On my business, on myself, and yes, on my next victims. I centered myself and pushed ahead.

"Okay, so you think I should open a new office? I guess whether I do it now depends on how willing I am to have Julie leave my side. I'm not, but she deserves a promotion."

"You're damn right she does," Joe exclaimed, shoving half a bagel topped with regular cream cheese and lox in his mouth. "You know, Brit, there is a gray area between control and delegation, and while this might be new territory for you, if the numbers work, you should seriously consider expanding. Yes, it'll be hard, and it'll be challenging, and some days you might wonder why you ever listened to this damned old fool. But you've got that entrepreneurial spark, my girl. And you've got grit. What we old-timers used to call moxie."

"Is that like bitchiness?" I winked at him.

He chuckled. "Not entirely. It's more measured than just attitude. It's attitude leavened with experience and tact. But you're getting there."

"Well then," I laughed and followed suit. The lox was so fresh, I swore it was salty enough to have just been fished. Then I dug a fork into the whitefish salad and put it in my mouth. My taste buds exploded. I couldn't figure out if it tasted so delicious because it'd been so long since I'd had any or if it was perfection. I didn't care. It really was amazing, and I made a mental note to ask Joe where he'd found all this great food.

We ate in silence for a while before my phone rang. It was Julie. I'd forgotten to tell her I would be in late. I swiped to answer.

"Jules, I'm so sorry!"

"Nah, no biggie. Hey, are you gonna be here by lunch?"

"Yeah, but I won't be eating. I'm at Joe's. Can I bring you food? He's got the whole Yom Kippur fast-breaking spread."

"Ohh! Yes please! I'll have to eat it when I get back, though. That's why I'm asking if you'll be here. I have a doctor appointment, and I'll be back a little late."

"Thanks for telling me. I should've called or sent a text. I'm so, so sorry. Really. I'll be back at some point. Is everything okay?"

"Of course! I'm just going to find out if there's any way I can have a baby of my own before exploring other options."

I squealed with joy. "Yay! I'm so happy you're set on having a family and so happy with Cody!"

Julie laughed. "Thanks. So I'll see you when I get back?"

"You will."

"Okay then. Talk soon. Love you."

"Love you too."

She hung up before I could end the call. I put my phone back in my purse and stared at my food, grinning stupidly. Joe looked at me and laughed.

"That's how I felt when my daughter first told me I was going to be a grandfather."

I made another squeaky noise and finished my brunch. Joe gave me tips on how to be supportive of Julie, no matter the outcome of today's appointment. He was used to handling and delivering bad news, being a plastic surgeon. For example, he frequently performed mastectomy reconstructions, and on rare occasions, the surgeon who removed the cancerous tissue had done so in such a horrible way, Joe couldn't fix it.

He offered to have his housekeeper pack up some food for me, but I insisted on doing it myself. She helped take care of him—which was a hefty job on its own—and his house, so I wasn't about to ask her to do something I was perfectly capable of doing on my own. He waved me off and laughed, finishing the last of the coffee in his mug. I pulled some plastic containers from their cabinet and set them on the table. Starting to place food in them, Joe insisted I take it all. He was right that he shouldn't have it in the house because he'd eat it all and probably have another heart attack from the cholesterol.

I packed all the food and put it in paper bags, setting them by the front door so I wouldn't forget to take them with me. Back in the kitchen, Joe and I hugged and joked that we needed to get together more often. He's not getting any younger and, contrary to popular belief, doesn't like living alone all the time. We talked about my coming over for dinner at least once a week, deciding we'd check our schedules and make a weekly plan.

I hugged him again and left. After I secured the bags of food in the back seats, I hopped behind the wheel and drove to the office. Lunch time traffic was in full effect. I parked in the office lot halfway through our scheduled lunch hour, taking the bags inside with me. Unlocking and opening the door was amusing and it was a shame the property owners wouldn't allow cameras because that would be fun to watch. I locked the door behind me, planning to unlock it once the lunch hour was over.

Once all the food was in the refrigerator, I pulled the pink paper messages Julie left me. There were a few clients who preferred speaking directly to me, while most were happy enough just being our clients and spoke to Julie about their needs or issues. One of the messages was from the accounting firm I'd placed the McLaughlin sisters with. I thought that odd and in no way coincidental. The girls were taken on full-time by the firm and I didn't believe in mere happenstance. I put that message on top of the pile.

I booted up my computer and readied all the programs I needed for the day by the time lunch was over. I unlocked the door and got to work, calling Bob over at the accounting firm.

Six

I WAS TRANSFERRED TO Bob, and we started off with the usual pleasantries. Turns out the girls actually left to contract for themselves. I wasn't sure if that was good or bad for me, considering they wouldn't have a set schedule. I did ask if anyone had problems with either of them, to which Bob responded with a negative. Their coworkers barely paid them any mind, and management and clients were satisfied with their work. They weren't exceptional, but they weren't awful. Average was the word he used.

When we got down to brass tacks, Bob needed two more temps—tax season was approaching. I entered his requirements in our system and posted the ad while still on the phone with him. I also sent him email confirmation, verifying he received it before ending the call.

I wanted to take the time to think about what the sisters leaving the firm meant for me, but the only conclusion I could come up with was I'd have to take them from their apartment. The last I knew, and verified through the DMV database, was they didn't own cars. Not even one between them. I guessed they Ubered or took the bus. The bus, however, only ran once an hour where they lived. I knew that from when I lived there. Uber made the most sense.

This was going to take longer than I wanted, but I was also grateful for that delay. It would give me time to plan, stalk, and not leave a trail. There was no indication that the cops were suspicious that a serial killer might be on the loose, and I planned to keep it that way. The only way to know for sure was to talk to Officer Stu Jones. We'd become friends after I shot Officer John Sweet for catching him breaking into my house. It was a long story I had no desire to talk about. He was in jail, and that was that.

I grabbed my phone and sent a text to Jones.

Long time! When do you wanna do lunch?

He didn't respond immediately, which was expected. I didn't know his schedule and never bothered to find out if his shift was permanent or rotated. I knew he'd text back when he had time.

I went back to returning calls and putting job requests in the database and on the job boards. I was on the phone when Julie came back and didn't even realize she'd returned. When I hung up, she came to my doorway looking hopeful.

"How'd it go?"

"Well, there's no hope of any kind of fertilization coming from Cody. My option for getting pregnant is a donor. Neither of us wants that, so we're talking about adoption. There are so many kids in foster care; it's sad and heartbreaking. We think that's the route we're gonna go, so we have an appointment with the local office of Department of Children and Families to talk to someone about adopting."

"That's amazing! I'm so proud of you."

"Yeah, me too. I have to say," Julie said as she walked to one of the chairs in front of my desk and sat down, "I'm actually happy about not getting pregnant."

We shared a laugh, and I got up, walked around my desk, and hugged her. The hug lasted about thirty seconds, and we both got back to work, Julie stopping in the kitchen to grab some of the food Osten made me take.

By the time the day ended, Julie had perked up a bit.

I didn't want the food in the fridge to go bad, so Julie and I divided it between us, making sure none would go to waste.

"Oh! I almost forgot. Yes, I'm down for a girls' night this weekend at your house."

"Perfect! We can figure out who's bringing what later in the week," I responded.

We waved bye and got in our own vehicles. I went straight home.

I parked in my garage, having no plans other than res earch—i.e., watching movies and such. The reprieve was a welcome one. I wouldn't have to hurry up making any decisions and could hunt at my leisure. I didn't expect anything too difficult or involved from the sisters. They, like the vast majority, were creatures of habit.

I went upstairs and changed into my pajamas before anything else. I wanted pure comfort before settling in for the night. My phone chimed downstairs, but I was in no rush to see who it was or what they wanted. I sauntered downstairs, feeding Minion, and ordering my own dinner before bothering to check my phone. It was Stu.

I'm late shift until Wednesday. Then I'm off 'til Saturday overnight.

His schedule was the strangest I'd even seen from a police department. It was four on, two off, four on, three off. Usually it was four on, three off, and that was that. Every other Friday, Saturday, Sunday off. But no, Tampa couldn't do anything the easy way. Hell, their dispatchers got their schedules two months in advance with rotating days off like this: five on, two off, and those two off were set. So, for example, I could work Monday, Tuesday, off Wednesday, Thursday, work Friday Saturday, Sunday. For a whole month straight. No thanks. Oh, and dispatchers worked eight-hour shifts. That's a big nope. I only knew this from trying to get a job dispatching a long time ago.

Well, you tell me which day. I'm available either day, I responded.

Okay, how about Friday then? My one normal schedule day ha-ha

Sure thing. Text me Friday and let me know time and place.

You got it, Brit. Miss you.

Miss you too, Stu.

Knowing Stu, we'd go to one of the sandwich shops around my office. He had a crazy work ethic and expected everyone else in the world to have the same one. If I haven't said the word enough yet, no. I worked hard to get where I was and continued to work hard, admittedly less so having Julie, but I've earned the time off. My company was in more than capable hands when I was away.

I sat on the couch and started a show I'd stopped in the middle of until the doorbell rang with my dinner. I kept swearing I'd cook more but wasn't about to start today. I got up, opened the door, signed, and went back to the couch. I didn't even need a fork—my food came with chopsticks.

I skipped back to the last part I remembered before getting up and dug in. The show gave me some ideas for future kills, but these sisters were special. They looked at Americans with such disdain and considering their glaringly obnoxious lack of artistic or intellectual appreciation for the culture that took them in, these philistine bitches deserved what I had in store for them. If they thought Americans were animals, they'd find out what that really meant. I had my "light bulb" idea and was more than ready to run with it. The remaining kill question was one of where I was running to.

Where could I make this possible?

Seven

I KNEW HOW I wanted the McLaughlin sisters to die and a general where. Disposal was another matter. First, I needed to find the exact, perfect place to kill them in the animalistic way they deserved. I went to bed figuring to pick at Stu's brain for just the right facility.

My daily weekday morning routine didn't vary terribly often, and today was not one of the days I'd need it to. Killing grounds and disposal came first, though I would likely stalk while figuring the rest out. That was me, who I was. I had tried many times to figure out what part was my favorite and was never able to. I enjoyed all of it. The thrill and ecstasy of the kill were something in their own rights. The stalk wasn't anywhere near as exciting but vital.

Work was work. I was so busy all day with calls and emails, by lunchtime I found myself letting out my breath as if I'd been holding it.

Julie noticed. "Are you okay?"

"I'm great, actually. I don't understand why I felt like I was holding my breath. Must be anxiety or something." I shook it off and shifted the conversation. "Everyone else got back to me. Friday night seems to be the one that works for them. What about you?"

Julie bit into her sandwich, chewed, and nodded. She swallowed, then said, "Yes. That works for me. What can I bring?"

I laughed. "You all ask me that, and the answer is always the same: wine. If you want to bring snacks, go ahead. We'll probably order dinner too." The girls knew that by snacks I meant cheeses they'd tried before and loved. I was on a constant search for cheese I'd never eaten and wanted to try it all. I supposed you could call me a cheese addict. I didn't think there was a rehab for it, and I had no plans to start one because I didn't see a problem. High cholesterol be damned.

We finished our lunches and went about finishing our work. It was finally starting to pick up again, causing me to consider opening another office. I started to lose track of how many times I considered this and decided to bite the bullet despite the complications and stress that would undoubtedly ensue. Any real estate purchase or lease was a royal pain in the ass and an absurd amount of stress and hassle. Even with the best real estate agent in the world, it was always a ludicrous time and money suck. *Something* always needed work, inspections, blah, blah, bullshit.

To counter the anxiety setting in, I decided to go home and get my stalk on. I almost let my truck run while I ran inside to change, but I was a bit paranoid when it came to my four-wheel child. I backed the Jeep in, got out, locked and armed it, and all but sprinted into the house and up the stairs. After changing, I fed my fur child and set out for Northdale.

Traffic was stupid at rush hour. Evening it was going north this time of day. If I didn't love my life so much, I'd have left it. But I did, so I wasn't going anywhere. Literally, at the moment. I was stuck in bumper-to-bumper traffic on North

Dale Mabry. The interstate wouldn't have been any better, and I despised tolls if other options were available.

At times I inched, and other times I could go half a mile. Regardless, it took almost an hour to get there. I pulled into the complex at the sign and hooked a right. The apartment was almost all the way in the back. As I backed into an empty parking space across from their second-floor apartment, I noticed Suk getting out of an Uber. The sun was setting right in my line of vision, but I already knew which number was theirs. I noted the time my phone had on its screen; I set my radio clock ten minutes fast. I waited about forty-five minutes longer before Jimin arrived home. Again, I noted the time.

Now came the fun part of watching and waiting, which I did until midnight before going home. Neighbors with dogs walked by and didn't even see me sitting in my Jeep. They were too busy on their phones, listening to earphones, or simply didn't care. I was grateful for that because it allowed me to work unhindered. I had yet to have some nosey jerk call the cops or think they were the tough guy to approach me and say something. People here largely minded their own business because they didn't care to be in someone else's. I learned that from living here. But the same was also true at my townhouse in South Tampa.

Once back home, I rinsed off and changed. I hated eating after 8 p.m., but I was starving, so I reheated last night's leftovers. I sat at the table to eat. I knew I was likely to add snacks after finishing if I sat on the couch.

I was tired from doing nothing. That always amazed me—how tired one could grow from simple surveillance or hours of not doing anything physical. I thought about it while I ate, coming up with no good reason why that happened. I threw out the plastic container when I finished, grabbed a couple treats for Minion, and went to bed. She purred as I handed the treats over before she climbed into my hair. We snuggled into blissful sleep.

I don't remember dreaming, but I also didn't recall the last time I did remember. I hopped out of bed feeling rested and went for my usual jog. It was earlier than my standard 6 a.m., so I started the coffee before showering. It was finished by the time I got out and dressed. I was able to sit and relax a bit before the day kicked my ass again. I watched the foreboding weather forecast; something about a front coming down and thunderstorms all day. I could go about stalking or I could come home and stay here after work. It was my choice. One I decided to make after work. Exhaustion and weather mattered not when there was stalking to be done. I just wasn't making any kind of premature decisions. After all, I had plans with the girls tomorrow night I had to prepare for.

I finished getting ready and worked almost nonstop until lunch and again until close. The day looked dreary though it was quite the opposite. Humid and wet, I felt like the fires of a volcano might be more comfortable. My decision was made. I was going home to clean and prep for girls' night. At least I could control the temperature inside my own house while I cleaned up the place. I'd go watch those bitches another day. Time was the one thing consistently on my side.

Eight

MINION SCREAMED AT ME when I got home. I had no idea why—when did I ever?—so I fed her and changed the water in her dish. She only drank filtered water because the water here was so harsh. She even drank from my glass. Spoiled was an understatement.

I went to change because I was not that woman who cleaned my house in heels. I preferred comfort, even if I was going to sweat. This wasn't the week for the cleaning people, so it was on me to make sure the carpets were vacuumed and everything wiped down. I kind of liked it this way because cleaning was a good release of stress and anxiety for me. Plus, I was in the guest room to clean and may have gotten new decorating ideas. Not that I was one for trends; I liked what I liked, and that was it.

I started upstairs and worked my way down, saving the carpeted stairs for last. I had this thing about tracking cat hair and dust bunnies through the house, so I always swept and vacuumed with sneakers on. It was a quirk I started when I moved out to live on my own. It was effective, too, so I saw no reason to run around cleaning in socks. I knew people who did and laughed at them for it. Socks while sweeping, mopping, vacuuming or otherwise cleaning floors was one of the most counterintuitive ways to clean.

Once the master was finished, the guest room was next. I worked backward downstairs until I reached the front door and stairs. Those lift-away vacuum things for smaller areas like stairs were so underrated. One of my favorite gadgets. Maybe I was getting old when I expressed my appreciation for appliances and such. So be it.

I got excited over a new toaster oven too. But those things were convenient. I was justified, dammit.

Once I was satisfied the house was picked up enough, I cleaned out the vacuum cleaner and put it away. Then I made some chickpea curry and watched a few movies. I hated the thought of running the dishwasher with so little in it, so I opted to wait until tomorrow night or Saturday to run it. We'd dirty enough dishes tomorrow night, so it wasn't a big deal to wait.

Minion had run off into some hidey spot when I started the vacuum and was just now coming back out of it. She reminded me of that photo of Albert Einstein plastered all over the internet with his hair standing in every direction, and I let out a cackle. Before feeding her, I gave her some extra treats for not attacking me after her trauma by vacuum.

I noticed the time wasn't much past 7 p.m., so I watched another two movies before going to bed. I was a sucker for a good superhero movie, so I chose *Iron Man* and *Iron Man 2*. I may also have had a crush on Robert Downey Jr. He made such a kick-ass comeback for himself too. Not that I expected to damn-near destroy myself the way he or so many others had, but if I did, I'd work even harder for a comeback like his. Hollywood wouldn't go near him for so long after his serious drinking and drug abuse. I'm just glad none of it took his life. I wondered if he was a cool human being.

These were the weird things I thought about when watching movies. Like how Hugh Jackman and Ryan Reynolds were always publicly making fun of each other but were the closest of friends. I loved seeing that celebrities were real people, especially when they were cool people. I've met some famous people through my work connections, and only sometimes was that old saying about never meeting your heroes true. It wasn't a constant; they're not all assholes. Believing that is like believing everything you see on social media. Do your own research so you can make a well-informed decision.

Take my nosey, old coot neighbor who, as I found out, called the property management company on me for Officer Jones stopping by in his patrol car to make sure I was okay after I shot former Officer John Sweet when he broke into my house. She didn't do her own research—like, oh, asking me maybe—and decided I'd pissed off the "unsavory types" as she called it. I wanted nothing more than to knock on her door and tell her the cop I was dating broke into my house and I shot him. But I didn't. It was none of her business. Regardless, my point was to maybe do some digging before you accused someone of being gang-associated. I still laughed when I thought about it—after the anger subsided, of course.

When both movies were over, I went up to bed, Minion pouncing onto me before I was even able to get comfortable.

Friday morning. I woke up excited for girls' night and took my jog easier than usual, considering I was getting back into work being busy again coupled with girls' night. It'd been a while, largely because I took my China trip during slow season. Our last girls' night was right after I got back. So I wasn't fully used to having my ass kicked and being up all night with the girls in the same day. I loved how my own mind thought I was older than I actually was. Next, I'd be telling myself I needed to be in an assisted living facility!

Showered and ready to get to the office a little early, I headed out the door, and my phone started singing. The caller ID told me it was Stu.

"Hey man! How are you?"

"I'm great, Brit! Thanks for asking. We still good for lunch today?"

"You know it. I hate to cut this conversation short, but text me time and place. I'm going in early to start looking at places for a new office in the unincorporated part of the county." I was trying to open the driver door and not drop my purse or phone, and to say my positioning was precarious was putting it gently.

"No problem. If you want me to scope anything out before lunch to save you some time, let me know."

"Thanks, Stu. I appreciate that. I'll let you fight my real estate agent about whether his assistant is going to scout or you will."

We both laughed. Stu knew my agent by reputation only. It wasn't a sparkling one either. He was good to me, though, and always sent his assistant to look at places for me so I didn't waste my time. He even had his assistant look for Julie's house. Which was still happening. Everything Julie liked photos of wasn't the best on the inside.

"Stu, I gotta go, I'm about to physically drop everything. You know, because I'm a huge klutz. . . yet nimble enough to sneak up on a burglar."

We laughed harder. "Okay. I'll text you soon. Good talk, Brit. Be safe."

"You too," I said and hung up. As I reached for the door handle, I dropped my purse. *And* I didn't have the phone between my ear and shoulder anymore. I sighed, laughed, picked it up, and climbed in.

By the time I arrived at the office, Julie was already there and working. I was ten minutes early. I went to put my key in the lock, and Julie waved a hand, signaling that was unnecessary. Pulling the door open, I wore a confused look.

"So, uh, why are you here so early, and why—"

Looking to my right, I saw why. Cody and some unknown older woman were talking on the couch. Julie beamed at me, and I took that as a good sign, continuing into my office and closing the door behind me.

I tried not to jump to any conclusions, but my excitement for them and happiness rose until I thought I would burst. I used the in-house messenger to ask Julie one question.

"Is that the social worker?"

While I impatiently waited for her response, I checked my email and organized my desk for the day. Even making a list of what to grab at Publix on the way home.

Ten minutes turned to twenty. I wanted to text her, but I also didn't want to be rude. It was, however, odd that they chose the office as a meeting place. For the life of me, I couldn't figure out why this woman wanted to watch Julie work. Then, I received a message back from Julie.

Maria would like to speak with you.

Oh, I typed, *coming.*

I stood, straightening myself, making sure neither I nor my office looked a mess, then walked to the door. I took a deep breath and opened it, wearing a nonchalant smile.

"Hello, Maria. Please come in." I stepped back to allow her entrance before closing the door behind her.

We shook hands and sat on the couch in my office.

"Hello," she started, "I'm Maria Velazquez from Social Services. I'll be handling Julie and Cody's adoption case."

She was a pleasant woman, fiftyish, salt-and-pepper shoulder-length hair. She stood maybe five foot five in her flats and was well groomed.

"It's wonderful to meet you, Maria. What can I help with?"

She looked at me, appraising me, for what felt like eternity. I saw she was trying to judge my character and if I'd lie on behalf of awful people who would commit unspeakable acts to the innocent. She must have decided I was worthy because she smiled a genuine smile.

Nine

"I CAN TELL YOU care deeply for Julie and Cody," she re-marked. "Most people don't ask how they can help. They ask what they can do. I like you, Britney. May I call you Britney?"

"You can call me whatever you'd like. I won't waste your time with a stupid dad joke."

She laughed. "If you could verify Julie's employment, to start."

I went to my computer, printed all of Julie's records, and handed them to her.

"Ms. Vazquez—"

"Please, Maria."

"Maria. Julie and Cody are great people. Julie is an exemplary employee and one I'd never want to lose. They have a dog called Applesauce, who is the sweetest and would protect anyone in their home. I know, I've been there. Both on the side being protected and simply meeting him."

I didn't want to offer more information than she asked; that could turn something good to something sour fast. I let her continue.

"Britney, what would you say is Julie's best quality?"

"Her heart. She's loyal, honest, and caring. She's not just an employee to me, but a friend. I can tell her anything without fear of judgment."

Maria smiled and nodded. "Teenagers would appreciate that." She scribbled on her notepad.

"I haven't been told much other than they were looking into adoption. If I may, I'd like to add if there's any kind of support needed, I can make sure it's provided. We do work with the best names in the city."

Maria looked at me, unsure what I meant. I nodded, and she then realized what I was getting at—if they adopted a special needs child, that child would be well taken care of. Her smiled broadened.

"Britney, you're too kind. And humble."

"What's mine is Julie's, including contacts. If extra care is necessary, rest assured it will be given."

"Britney, may I ask why you don't have your own children?"

I laughed. "I do, but she's not human. I decided early in life that I didn't want to place the burden of an ever-barbarous society on an innocent. I couldn't justify being the person who brought another innocent life into such turmoil. I don't see it as fair. However, I respect those who bring a child into the world and play an active role in their lives."

Maria looked at me like I was buttering her to eat her. I wasn't. Those were my honest views on having children. Besides, Minion was about as well behaved as an infant.

She rose from her seat and straightened her suit. I followed, placing my hand in front to shake. I didn't expect the hug she wrapped me in.

"Thank you," she whispered, a tear falling onto my shoulder.

"There's no need for thanks. I try to be as…rational as possible."

Maria let go, wiped her face, and picked up her things. "We'll be in touch."

I nodded, opening the door for her. Julie was at her desk, and Cody looked downright worried. Maria shook my hand again, then shook Cody's and Julie's in turn before leaving. Once Maria was safely out of range, Julie ran to Cody, and I joined them. They looked at me, waiting to hear the words our conversation contained.

I wanted to joke with them, but this was too important a topic, and I didn't have the heart. I launched into the two questions she asked and my honest replies. Julie started crying, and I was sure Cody couldn't say "thank you" any more in thirty seconds.

They both broke into smiles and hugged me.

I loved them; I wasn't going to hurt them. This meant too much to all of us. I enjoyed being an auntie and looked forward to another child—who's not mine—to spoil. Cody wanted to celebrate, so I agreed to close the office down early as long as Julie and I were on time for girls' night. Cody was reluctant but knew we had this planned for a week now.

Instead of going to anywhere we usually went, I chose a lesser-known Mexican joint in St. Pete. Happy hour was earlyish but not happening when we arrived. Not that it mattered anyway. This was a special occasion. We were marking the beginning of a long and arduous journey, one that would test our resolves and tolerance. Dealing with government in any capacity was never a delight.

We ordered so many fresh homemade tacos Julie was afraid she wouldn't have room for cheese from the cheese plate. I laughed. I did the same thing. I said I had no room, then proceeded to eat half the cheese plate myself. I'd pay for it the next day, but it was cheese, and it was my life. I did what I wanted with it.

Cody attempted to order a round of margaritas until I told him tequila made me turn into a green cartoon character.

He thought I was talking about SpongeBob's friend with the dildo nose. I choked on my chorizo taco, and Julie spit her iced tea out through her nose. Yes, this was my life. I wouldn't have traded it for anything.

I excused myself to go to the restroom and handed the server a crisp one hundred-dollar bill to cover our food and tip. She stammered, blushed, and tried to give it back. I gently pushed her hand back to her and asked that she not tell my friends. She gratefully accepted and thanked me profusely. Julie and Cody were so dear to me, I wanted to give them things I wasn't always able to have at their age. Not that I was more than five years older than either of them, but I did remember living on ramen for too long. Of course, I was really trying to make sure my credit was good enough to afford a house; I detested apartment living and still do.

As I sat back at the table, the server brought me another unsweet tea with a nod of appreciation. Cody attempted to ask for the check, and for a minute, the server looked nervous, then told him it was on the house. He was baffled, and so was Julie. Until she realized the truth. If I was able to accurately explain the daggers mixed with genuine thanks in her eyes, I would.

We'd all arrived in separate vehicles—which I thought was weird—so we departed that way too. Julie called me from her hands-free option on her phone.

"Brit," she scolded, "for real?" Her voice raised an octave or two.

"Yes. Don't even think of trying to pay me back either. Just be there tonight and have fun. You mean so much to me, and I want you to be happy. I'm not asking you to let me do things for you two or the child either. Auntie Brit's got this. I want your kid to have more than I did—of everything, especially love."

Julie stifled her argument when I said that. Then I heard sniffling.

"Julie, stop that. Get yourself together, and I'll see you in a few hours."

"Okay. Thank you, Brit. From the bottom of my heart."

"I love you, girl. No thanks needed," I said, disconnecting the call.

I drove home, bopping my head to some pop music I'd rather not admit to. I was all smiles, even when I stopped off at Publix, and finally parked in my garage. I danced around the house tidying up and feeding Minion. I pulled the things from the closet in the guest room that I'd been saving for Julie's engagement and bachelorette parties. It wasn't quite time to use any of it, but I also had notes on things I still wanted to get. A pin-the-nose-on-SpongeBob's-friend game was now top of the bachelorette party list.

By the time I'd managed to get it all put neatly back, my doorbell rang.

"Coming!" I called, walking in socks to answer it.

I looked through the peephole to see someone I wasn't expecting.

Ten

Sighing, I unlocked and opened the door.

"What's up?"

"Nothing. Well, I guess something. Did you block my calls after blowing off lunch?" Stu looked hurt.

"No, I—wait, you called? I didn't get anything missed," I said half jogging to my phone. "Come in." When I got to my phone inside my purse, sure thing, there were five missed calls and three texts. All from Stu.

"Shit! We were supposed to have lunch, and I'm the worst friend."

Stu laughed. "You are not. I was worried is all."

"Stu, are you still with what's-her-name?" I asked grabbing him a beer from the fridge and pouring myself a glass of wine.

"Uh…"

I handed him the bottle, and he tipped it to me in cheers, then chugged it.

"Is everything okay between the two of you?" I asked, sitting next to him.

He turned to me and set his bottle on a coaster on the coffee table, a look of somber consternation on his face. "No. We've been broken up for months. She isn't thrilled that you and I are friends—"

"So she's insecure." I sipped my wine.

"You could say that."

"I did. And it's not a matter of question. I'm insecure too. As I'm sure you are. It's nothing to be embarrassed about."

"I know that, and yes I am, but she won't agree. I tried to tell her it's nothing to worry about. She left and hasn't spoken to me since." Stu picked his bottle back up, took a swig, and hung his head.

"There will be none of that bullshit in this house. Tonight is girls' night, but I think we can make an exception for a friend in a rut," I smirked, holding my glass out in toast. He clinked his bottle, and we drank.

The girls arrived one by one, Stu being too gracious and answering the door while I was in the kitchen cutting up various cheeses. The girls all poured glasses and chitchatted, Heather and Danielle even physically dragging Stu in with us. Julie was the last to arrive, opening the door and yelling something I couldn't understand over us.

"Jules, repeat that?"

She came into the kitchen and exclaimed, "*Now* we can get the party started! Oh! Hey, Stu! Uh, is everything okay here?"

"Yeah, I'm just one of the girls tonight," he told her, taking the bags from her hands.

"Girl, what did you bring? We have more than enough."

"Sure, but we all agreed to bring something." She stuck her tongue out at me like a child would and made noises. I laughed so hard I almost sliced myself open.

"Well, if there's blood on the cheese, everyone can blame Julie," I laughed.

Stu made sure we all had drinks before raising his bottle in toast.

"To Britney, one of the coolest chicks on the planet. Probably one of the best people I know, aside from yours truly." He smirked that adorable, devilish half grin of his. "Cheers!"

I blushed. Hard. The only other person to ever make me blush like that was Devin. I had to have been getting hormonal in my ripe age of twenty-seven.

I lifted my glass, nodding to everyone. "Thank you all for being the best friends a girl could ever hope for. Cheers!"

If they only knew the other side of me.

We spent the first few hours chatting and talking about any recent developments since the last time we'd seen each other. All developments except, of course, the Birthday Girls from The Pub. We ate cheese—some of it super stinky—drank wine, and had a great time. The addition of Stu wasn't bad either. He seemed to liven things up a bit. It may have been because he'd thrown back more than a few beers, or it could have just been him. I never really knew him outside of a casual, friendly lunch. This was a treat.

I mentally threatened myself to not find him charming enough to want to sleep with him. NO MORE COPS. Friendzone was the only acceptable place. I didn't want to have to shoot another busybody, let alone a cop. I wanted to feel bad about John, but I couldn't. I still felt a little vulnerable from that day. Violated even. I'd rekeyed the locks and was still debating cameras, but that bastard was still in prison, so I wasn't terribly concerned.

The girls were ready to move our gathering to the living room, Julie cutting up more cheese, Sarah and Danielle pulling more bottles from the fridge, and Heather doing...Was she singing and marching like a parade director? I burst out laughing, spitting on Stu in the process. He wiped it away with his sleeve and winked at me. That was weird. Drunky must be horny. I wanted to ask him why he waited so long to tell me about the breakup. Maybe it was something best left alone.

Standing up from the kitchen table, I motioned for Stu to follow. He stood, too, then grabbed another beer before motioning for me to go first.

Sarah, Heather, Julie, Danielle, and Kristen were already spread out between the couches, with the bottles of wine and cheese plate on the coffee table. Stu sat on the couch next to Julie, and I sat in the overstuffed chair. We all told stories and laughed. Stories about kids and their antics, coworkers, crazy clients. Nothing was off limits for them to get off their chests tonight. I didn't have anything to get off my chest; I had thinking to do.

The night was quite enjoyable. Stu was a hit, and as we all went to our separate rooms for the night, Stu vowed to stand guard by sleeping on the couch. I pulled an extra pillow from my bed and a blanket from the closet. By the time I got back to the living room to give them to him, Stu was out cold, gun on his hip, exposed by the buttons having been undone on his shirt. He was a much better-looking specimen than the Stu Jones I'd first met.

I sighed and went to my bedroom, changing and climbing under the covers with Minion.

"What a shame," I said before I fell into an alcohol-induced slumber.

I woke to a shrieking smoke alarm and rolled my eyes and snorted. I threw the covers off me like in the movies, only sloppier, and brushed my teeth. I pulled my robe on as I padded down the stairs. Smoke wafted up, but so did the smell of bacon and…Was that burned egg?

Sarah, Kristen, and Danielle were hysterically laughing at the table, sipping their coffee. I stopped in the doorway, amused by the show.

Julie was trying to help a hungover Stu make the eggs, but her scolding him about mixing beer in the eggs made me laugh—and throw up a little in my mouth. I walked to the coffee pot, poured a mug, and set it on the table by Danielle. Then I went to the stove. I carefully placed my hands on Stu's shoulders and guided him to the table with everyone else. That's when I noticed Heather wasn't there. I pushed the button on the smoke alarm to make it stop its terrible noise.

Once it was silent, I asked how Heather was still asleep.

Sarah sipped her coffee and swallowed. "She had to work. One of the clients she talked about last night called her. Something about an emergency." She made air quotes when she said emergency.

I rolled my eyes. I knew that feeling too well. Nine times out of ten, it wasn't an emergency. In Heather's case, it very well could be—she was a physical therapist—but with Sarah saying it was one of the clients talked about only a few hours prior, I didn't believe it.

"So dude thinks he's gonna get in her pants," Stu stated, amused.

It was funny. Stu was a cop, so there wasn't much he hasn't seen or heard. Yet he still looked for the funny to lighten the darkness. Kind of like me. I was dark, sure, but in sad times, I tried to find the silver lining or the funny. If there was one mood I hated being in, it was a funk.

In almost no time, Julie had the pan cleaned out and eggs not *en flambé*. I went over to the stove to help and was shooed away like a child. So I grabbed the coffee pot, refilled everyone's mugs, and started to make a fresh pot. Five people and twelve cups of coffee. It disappeared as quickly as a football team's Gatorade. Not that we weren't nursing various states of being hungover. But coffee alone was never enough. We needed grease, and Julie knew it.

She placed a plate of fresh bacon from the oven in front of us, soaked in its own grease from baking it on a sheet pan. This was my protégé, and I couldn't have been prouder in that moment. She could take care of five hungover adults, including herself. I was sure she could handle a kid, and I couldn't wait for that.

I tried again to help, and she slapped my hand away. I was now the unofficial coffee bitch. I topped off everyone's mugs again. So many times was I up and down from my seat, my thighs felt like I'd done a hundred squats. No pain, no gain.

By the time I'd started the fourth pot, breakfast was ready. Someone ran out to the Publix around the corner and picked up a dozen bagels and cream cheese. There was also a carafe of Bloody Mary along with some sausage and sliced, smoked gouda. We all dug in, hardly speaking except asking someone to pass something. Once we finished, I started clearing the table. Everyone helped, bringing me a mug or plate or both. I loaded the dishwasher and started it.

The girls left, hugging and kissing me as they did, leaving me alone with Stu.

Eleven

STU AND I STARED at each other awkwardly. He started to speak and stopped.

I did the same thing.

It was like one of those movies where both parties are secretly but-not-so-secretly in love with each other. Except I was not in love with Stu. Devin was my toy and I his. Stu didn't fit into that equation. Even if I wanted him to replace Devin. But I respected Stu too much to have to kill him. I just couldn't do it. John Sweet was a lesson learned.

Stu cleared his throat. "I should get going too." He checked his hip, that his gun was securely holstered, and hugged me on his way to the door. He turned the knob, paused, and looked back at me.

"Thanks, Brit. You really are a good friend. I needed a night like that. Lunch next week?"

"You know it. This time, I'll let you know if I can't make it."

We laughed and Stu left. I stood there a minute, confused. I really liked the guy but too much to ever have to kill him. He could be the first person I'd ever thought I might have to kill and actually feel true guilt and remorse for. I wouldn't allow that. The city—the world even—would lose a man too good for it, and it would be my fault. No.

Everyone I cared about was much safer in the darkness I carefully created; my secrets were just that. The blood on my hands would not be that of anyone I cared about as long as I had a say. I was now feeling fidgety, so I went up to change for a jog.

It was a decent enough day, with the sun in and out of the clouds. A light breeze flowed across my face. I jogged harder until it burned, forcing thoughts of Stu from my veins.

What I needed was to stalk and plan. I figured out the kill a little while ago. The trouble was when and where.

Post-jog showered and changed, I decided to see what the sisters did on weekends. The parking lot was fairly empty considering the weather. It wasn't nice enough to be in the pool, but some people were, while others were out and about. A lot of people were probably down in Ybor or doing one of the numerous outdoor activities available around town and beyond. It was a great theme park day.

I parked a few spots over from the last time I was here. There was movement on their patio: both women sitting out on chairs, drinking from mugs, and laughing. It was just about lunchtime, and my stomach was grumbling. I was getting really bad at the stalking and food thing. All I had was half a case of water in the back. I planned to sit here at least until dinner, which was now going to feel longer than it actually was. I made a note in my phone's note app. It was a single word. *Food*. I hated making real notes when it came to anything related to my hobby. Notes showed premeditation, which I couldn't even try to deny. But notes would also get me caught. Sure, I could change the app permissions, but I had the feeling the almighty Android gods had their ways. Just as Apple did.

Time dragged, and the sisters didn't seem to do much. They walked around the apartment or didn't move for long periods of time. I didn't hear laughter if they were watching a funny TV show, no yelling. Nothing. Their windows were open too. They hadn't come out of the front door for even a walk. I was beginning to think they were some of the most boring people temporarily still alive until they actually did come out again.

Not onto the patio, but through the front door. Dressed like pirate hookers. Mind blown, I sat there wondering what the hell was going on. It wasn't Gasparilla, the local holiday full of parades and drunk people in the streets downtown. They must have been going to a costume party or something. Convention season had started, but the only one I knew of anywhere close wasn't today.

I was amused by their getups. So much so, holding in the laughter began to hurt my ribs and tears fell like small waterfalls. Suk was wearing fishnets, surprisingly cute boots, and the typical black/red/white dress and corset thing. It was strategically torn, exposing just enough skin to entice anyone she pleased. Jimin rocked matching boots, torn fishnets, and a matching costume that substituted the red for purple. I never understood the pirate love. I knew enough history to have a measure of recognition for them, but also disdain. These two were not Jack Sparrow.

The longer they stood out here waiting for their ride, the more it physically hurt to stifle the laughter. I was too close to them and even with the windows up, they'd hear me. A Toyota sedan pulled up bearing the Uber logo in the front windshield, and they got in. It wasn't quite dinner time, but I was so hungry, I would've considered eating human if it was offered. I waited a few more minutes and pulled out of the complex, headed for Steak 'n Shake. I was craving a royale burger meal. I went inside to eat knowing how greasy their burgers were and wasn't risking getting it all over the inside of the Jeep.

Satisfied and full, I got in my Jeep and headed home. Southbound traffic sucked, no matter the time or day. I constantly bitched about it, and there was nothing that can really be done unless the county wanted to start banning new residents. Which won't happen. Ever. Do counties anywhere do that?

It was also good for me because it meant more business and more reasons for more killing. So long as I didn't screw up. And I'd been doing too much of that, as far as I was concerned. I was still lacking a kill site and disposal method by the time I got home. I was in the mood for a documentary, so I put one on from YouTube. As I was ready to vomit, I felt like a cartoon character with the light bulb above my head. I had my kill roughly planned out. Anyone for long pig?

It's sad what we do to animals, and I thought I might have sworn off meat. I didn't, though. I went to Publix and picked up a steak. At least the meat I cook at home will be humanely treated while they're alive. Sadly, even the humane way of slaughter didn't seem humane. I may have gotten angry about the atrocities against the innocent, and I wouldn't apologize for being a carnivore. The only meat I didn't eat was pork chops. I'd eat anything else at least once. Twice if I liked it.

I cooked it like I'd seen in a Gordon Ramsay video. Yes, I loved him. I could watch his videos all day. Maybe that's what I'd spend my night doing. There was no such thing as knowing too much about how to cook good food. My dad taught me a lot, and I still call him asking how to make certain things I grew up with. Someone else's recipes for that kind of thing wouldn't suffice for me.

So I seared the steak in my cast iron, made a salad, and enjoyed every bite. I'm sure I tried to thank Mr. Ramsay aloud while I chewed. After washing the dishes, I wiped out the skillet, put it away, and went to relax and watch more Gordon Ramsay videos. I even had a notebook dedicated to his videos alone. I also had one for Anthony Bourdain. I loved both of those men so much. Even more because they shared tips on making good food. I still shed tears over the loss of Mr. Bourdain, and I didn't usually get upset over celebrities. Hell, I rarely got upset over people I knew.

The more videos I watched, the hungrier I got—again. It was pure psychology that I was full and digesting while believing I was hungry again. I was satiated. And my eyelids were growing heavier the longer I watched and took notes. Maybe it was time for bed, but it was too early. Even if I napped, it'd fuck with my sleep schedule. Not that I had one, but I tried to keep one.

The next thing I knew, I opened my eyes, and it was dark outside.

Twelve

THE CLOCK READ MIDNIGHT. Damn, I slept a while. I felt pretty damned good too. Awake enough to properly prep for a stalk session. So I did. I made a smoothie and grabbed some snacks that weren't messy and jumped in my Jeep.

Up in Northdale, the lights were on, and I doubted the girls were home yet. They were definitely enjoying their party the night I had decided to kill them. I wanted to take a peek around their building, so I did. The streetlights that lit the sidewalks were dimmer than I remembered. That wasn't a bad thing. At least not for my activities. Slinking around and checking the place out was easier this way.

I didn't see anything that would cause an issue aside from the stairs to their apartment. Not a single neighbor looked out their windows or said a word to me. This is what I remembered. I wished my current neighborhood was like this, but there was always that one person. Lately, she had actually left me alone, so I guess I couldn't bitch too much.

Getting a better idea of the immediate layout and neighbors was a priority. The complex never installed cameras either, which would bother me if I lived here. The neighborhood hadn't gone to total shit yet, but it wasn't the best anymore.

Surveillance and foot survey completed, I hopped back into my Jeep. I'd only turned the ignition on when the sisters came back from their night of pirate hookering. I watched them stumble out of the Uber Hyundai sedan and up the stairs to their apartment. I had to laugh because I was sure this was what I looked like that drunk. Once they'd closed the door, I left. The McLaughlin sisters may not have been everything I wasn't sure I hoped for, but they further proved they liked their alcohol. This would make the ketamine dosage a whole lot less than the 3 cc's I used on Brody. Shit, between the two of these girls, I *might* use 1 cc. And the same syringe. Diseases didn't spread when you were dead.

Pulling out, the front of my Jeep was almost hit by someone speeding around the corner. That driveway in and out of the complex was kind of a pain anyway. Only genius engineers do that shit. Whether the driver who damn near got their ass handed to them in court—it wasn't like I could've beaten them to death and not been caught again—was paying attention or not didn't matter either. I once watched a Prius land itself on a boulder by the leasing office because he underestimated the curve, and he was paying attention. I honked, he waved, end of incident.

Heading home, I was starting to feel a little tired again. This was a welcome sign in that I wouldn't screw with my sleep schedule too much. Again, it didn't mean much because night was also when I KKD—kidnap, kill, dispose.

At home, I changed and crawled back into bed. The last pieces of this kill puzzle would soon reveal themselves. I fell asleep with a smile.

A few hours' nap and I was right as rain. I didn't eat anything I'd taken with me for my late-night stalk, so I decided to skip my jog. I did drink a lot of coffee, though. There was a new brand I wanted to try, so I finished the one-and-a-half pots the bag yielded. I'd already placed the order for the new stuff online and wasn't planning to need another pot until my order arrived. Minion interrupted my thoughts with a scream and a headbutt. I hadn't yet fed her, so I'm sure that's what she was getting at.

I hung out around the house in my pajamas for most of the rest of the day. I did put human clothes on for my evening trip to Publix but then changed back into my pajamas. Later on, I made myself an amazing smoothie that filled me up more than expected and let me avoid making dinner.

I felt pretty okay about not being terribly active today. I'd needed a day like this. That evening, I watched half of a season of one of my favorite Netflix shows before bed. I knew I could take my time watching it because they always dropped a series at the end of the third season, regardless of what fans wanted. But we're the idiots who still paid for the subscription. Maybe I'd start looking for DVDs of shows.

I made myself laugh at that thought. Despite myself, I put Netflix on to go to sleep. I also had no desire to own fourteen seasons of the show I put on that should have ended at ten, but that's network TV. After flipping through about twelve or so episodes, I settled on one that would be my lullaby and closed my eyes.

Monday again. My favorite day of the week. No, I really mean that. The day typically went by so fast that I often wondered where it went. Tuesdays were my nemesis. They dragged like a dial-up internet connection.

At the office, the phones rang like crazy; even I was answering calls. By lunchtime, I'd had enough. I called our commercial realty agent and set him to work. After lunch, I posted ads for two new employees, one to work under Julie and one to work under me. I refused to use the word *replace* because Julie was irreplaceable. She was, however, promotable. I called her into my office just before we closed for the day.

"Jules—" I hesitated. I didn't want to be without her day to day, but she deserved this, and we needed to expand. At least I could have her train a new assistant for me. She was waiting for me to speak again. "Jules, I posted ads for new employees, and I have Kevin looking for a second office. Do you want your own office?"

Her face turned bright red, and she tried to answer me, but no sound came out. She tried again. A meek voice came out. "Are you sure? I mean, I love being here with you, and I wouldn't say yes if you didn't want me to."

"I'm asking you because you deserve it and I trust you. You know the clients, and you're great at what you do. Make my day and say you'll take it. Please?"

"Can I think about it?"

"Sure. You'll have a say in the location of the new office too. I just want you to be happy, whatever you decide."

I walked around my desk and hugged her. "Jules, please don't feel pressured to say yes. If you'd rather stay here with me, I'd love that also. I'd like for you to be the first interview and part of the second. We both need to be comfortable with new direct employees."

"I agree. I'm going to see how Cody feels about it and get back to you."

"Tell him it comes with a raise." We both laughed. "That may help him decide. My main concern is your personal happiness. Always has been."

"Thanks, Brit. I really appreciate that. I love you so much."

"I love you. Now, what do you say to getting out of here for the night?"

"Oh, hell yes."

With that final sentiment, we packed up and locked the office. Tomorrow was another day. One that would bring who-knows-what insanity now that I had job postings up for Passing Through.

Thirteen

I WASN'T SURE HOW well I called it or not, but holy shit. The voicemail was full, and my email was…Well, luckily only one notification per site. Since I'd specified to reply to the ad only, those who called to follow up in the same twenty-four-hour period were discarded. If anyone knew about being desperate, I did. I've done the same, largely because online ads didn't give a direct email address but some people gave phone numbers or company names or even direct emails.

Julie and I cross-referenced our lists and went on to discard the matches. All I asked was that prospective employees follow damned directions. Cross-referencing pulled out about twenty people. Then I went through the sites I posted on and printed out the résumés that caught my attention, labeling them with position applied for. I handed those over to Julie. She decided whom she wanted to screen via phone call and trashed the rest.

By lunch, we were both famished. Who knew screening applicants would be so exhausting? I did. And this wouldn't be the last time. Especially if Passing Through kept growing. We ran across the street to Wawa to grab food and caffeine in the form of energy drinks. I was so distracted; I didn't even notice Julie snuck in line in front of me. She even managed to pay for her lunch and our dessert. Tastykake Butterscotch Krimpets. What a treat!

After we ate, I stared at my pack of Krimpets and drooled. I wanted to savor them, and our time was less than that would allow. I sat them on my desk, vowing to enjoy them for breakfast tomorrow.

Julie found that amusing to the point of tears and hiccups. She just didn't get it. My family was from where Tastykake started, same as Wawa. Even my dad and birth mother were from that area. When they moved here, they instilled a love for proper hoagies and other foods, like cheese steaks.

Here in Tampa, we were blessed by a Chester County native to have an amazing cheese steak joint, complete with proper Amoroso's rolls. I was told by a friend I could order fresh rolls online, and she wasn't messing around. Plus, Cheez Whiz. Life was complete-ish. I had my proper cheese steaks, and really, that was all that mattered. Outside of that one restaurant with two locations, I wasn't getting a real cheese steak unless I made it myself. I did enjoy making them, so that worked.

By the end of the day, Julie and I had narrowed somewhere around sixty applicants down to ten. I knew I could pull the ads whenever I wanted, but we always gave people we left messages for twenty-four hours to return them. If they didn't call us back, they also went into the discard pile—aka trash. Tomorrow would give us brand new applicants to sort through. We had a system—er, I had a system—that worked well enough.

"Hey Jules, want to go for drinks?" I called from my desk as I was packing up for the day.

"Nah, I'm beat. I never fully understood what you go through until now," she laughed, somewhat uncomfortable. I was beginning to think she was going to turn down the promotion, which was a fifty-fifty split of emotions for me. On one side, I'd get to have her here with me every day. On the other, she'd be in my position a few miles north.

"Brit?"

"What's up?" I asked as I walked into the reception area.

"I'm torn. I want the promotion, but I want to stay here with you." Julie let out a heavy sigh, one she'd been waiting to give into all day.

"I want you to do what's best for you, not me, Julie." I meant every word, but I didn't have to believe I did. I was a selfish person at times. Now was one of those times.

"Can I try the other office and come back?"

I don't think I'd ever been asked such a reasonable question before. I momentarily stumbled over my own thoughts trying to formulate an answer.

"Absolutely! And you keep the raise if you want to come back to this location. I'm not an asshole like that. Jules, you've earned it all and then some."

"Thank you so much, Brit." Julie's face lit up like I'd only seen once before. "You're the best boss and friend anyone could ever hope for!"

She about jumped on me to wrap me in the hardest hug she had yet to give me. Then her shoulders bobbed.

"Don't cry, Jules. It'll all work out. Promise." I rubbed her back as I spoke.

"I'm not scared or worried." She stepped back half a step, revealing a smile I'd only ever seen in cartoons. "You really are the best. Thank you so much, Brit."

"Girl, please. I care about you. I adore you. I want you to have everything you've ever wanted and more. I'll never have a daughter, and we're too close in age anyway, but I want more for you than I had."

We both cried, then laughed at ourselves. We hugged again and parted ways. I was sad she might be leaving me but proud of the woman she'd become in such a short period of time. Julie was closer to me than my other friends, regardless how long we'd known each other. She spent the most time with me. And I was able to hide from her too. I was as disturbed by this as I was pleased.

By the time I got home, the sun was almost fully behind the trees. Even though I lived on the west coast of Florida and the sun set later than the east coast of the state, it was still almost depressing. Just 5 p.m. and getting dark. The silver lining was that the oppressive, Hades-like summer would be here soon, and I could go back to bitching about the weather for almost ten months. But hey, I'd have sunshine until 8 p.m. because Congress sucks and wants the Sunshine State to suffer Daylight Savings. My electric company didn't hate DST, but anyone who paid those power bills seemed to.

I laughed something evil. I was surrounded by retirees in my neighborhood. Some were great; the majority of them weren't. I was grateful that majority left me the hell alone. I left them alone, too, but they talked to each other and kept pushing to do illegal things, like releasing a newsletter with phone numbers and new owners' info and…No. Their ludicrous requests made me laugh.

There was a note on my front door from the same strange people I had just been thinking about. It was a newsletter of "community events." I cackled so loud it echoed. I turned to see if anyone heard and looked out their windows. A few people did, and I laughed again. I trashed the paper once I'd made it into the house. *Assholes will never learn that they're wasting their time because no one cares except them.* Did I care if a child molester moved in? Fuckin' A right I did. I may not have kids, but my friends did, and I'm sure I've already established where I stand on harming the innocent.

I think my favorite part of all their bullshit was that they didn't have the slightest clue who I was. They knew who I was when I interacted with them and that was it.

Minion tripped me as I paced, lost in my own amused mind. I suppose it was feeding time. After I poured hers, I made mine. Grilled chicken avocado salad. I found myself wishing I had some fresh bread from Publix. Their bakery was amazing. I'd have to remember to keep some fresh bread on hand consistently. It was always a good thing to have. Like tortilla chips and salsa, it was good if someone stopped over, or even as part of a meal.

After dinner, I inspected the contents of the safe in my closet. I needed nylon rope for what I had planned for the sisters. My bag would be significantly lighter than usual, consisting of gloves, ketamine and syringe, nylon rope, and a knife. I didn't have a preferred knife, though the thought of maybe finding one intrigued me. I saw a shopping trip in my future. To an inconspicuous gun or hunting shop. Somewhere without cameras. And I didn't want to spend much; I'd be trashing the knife once I killed the girls.

Fourteen

I FOUND I WASN'T in a mood to follow those two around until after I decided where the kills and disposals would happen. I knew what I wanted, how I wanted it. This could very well be the method to almost skeeve me out. Almost. I knew I wouldn't want to die in any way I've already killed. I also knew I wouldn't want to drown or a few other things. I had an active imagination and could sometimes feel the things I thought about or did to others. Honestly, if I had my choice of deaths, I think I'd choose the absolute fear of skydiving with a shit parachute that didn't open. Some would see that as justice if they knew I'd killed their family or whomever. I was morbid and I wouldn't apologize for it.

I drove around town aimlessly, looking for the kind of place I needed. It was a place I wouldn't have to worry about cleaning up. There was a local place, but I didn't want to risk the possibility of bringing negative attention to an already persecuted community.

Back home, I ran a search of where else I could pull this off. I clicked the fifth or so link down the page. Bingo. Now I was concerned the ketamine might kill them before I could. But they were small people, and I doubted very much they'd wake up in transit. I should pick up some smelling salts too. Just in case.

I changed for bed and crawled under the blankets. Pushing the button for Netflix, it hit me: The place I was taking the girls to was dual purpose. I could kill them *and* dispose of their bodies. Now I was too excited to sleep. I still didn't feel like stalking them, though. They were quite boring. But now that I had two-thirds of KKD, I needed the last third. Not tonight. Tonight was Johnny Depp as Willy Wonka and a text to Devin.

Within twenty minutes, he was at my door.

"I've missed you," he smiled as I opened the door.

He stepped in and kissed me so hard I was almost unable to close and lock the door behind him. He assisted with that, and we were back on our way to ripping each other's clothes off on the way up the stairs.

I didn't realize the energy I'd let build up. By the time we were exhausted, we'd both been satisfied twice. I somehow managed to crawl out of bed and rinse off, Devin with me. Then we went back to bed and passed out.

My vision was blurry when I woke up. Last night was unbelievable, the best we'd had yet. I didn't want to give this up for Stu. And I didn't want to bother keeping track of more than one special friend.

That's when it got complicated. I learned that back in college. Add that to the fact that I was mid-plan for killing the McLaughlin sisters. Nope. No, thank you. Too much could go too wrong too easily. This would be my first dual kill, and I wasn't playing games with it. I liked life freedom and had zero dreams of prison.

Devin said something to me. I didn't hear him, just the sound of his voice. Like I'd been drugged. Which, technically speaking, we both had been. I rolled my head so I could look at him.

"I said I'm skipping this morning's class. I feel so weak from last night. What got into you?"

"Darlin', I wish I knew," I laughed. "This could be our every encounter if I did."

He kissed my cheek and laid his head on my chest. We lay like that for what felt like hours. When I turned my head, I about jumped out of bed.

It was 7 a.m. on the clock. I kissed his head and gently slid out from under him.

"Where are you going?"

"I have a company to run, Devin. You can stay if you want, but I've got an expansion in progress and interviews scheduled for today."

He looked hurt. I felt a pang of—what was that? Guilt?—as I turned toward the bathroom. I mentally berated myself. No attachments; that was my rule. Not just for him but for me, too. That rule sure looked like it was hitting a breaking point. He'd missed me more than I anticipated. Maybe I'd missed him—meaning more than just his body. I didn't see how that was possible considering we spent way more time in bed than in conversation. It was just sex; I had to keep believing that.

"Devin," I called as I turned the shower on.

"Yeah?"

"I'm not sure we should see each other for a while. I know this has been kind of a semiregular thing, and I'm not saying I don't enjoy every inch of you and your mind. I'm just so busy and under so much pressure…" I lied and hated it. What the fuck was happening to me?

"Brit, I understand. I was starting to think I could use some time away too. I won't lie; I am starting to form an attachment to you. I know that's your rule, and I agree with it. Neither one of us wants a relationship right now. Maybe we should take time to figure out what it is we want from each other."

Well shit. I wasn't expecting anything remotely close to a rational human answer from him. The last time I was with a guy, he accused me of being a murderer and broke into my home. Then the jerk called me from jail to, to, to what? Prove his obsession? I didn't know, and I didn't care to ever find out.

But Devin. Oh, sweet, talented, smart, hung Devin. I wanted him to be there every time I needed his talents. It was all so bittersweet.

Devin came into the bathroom as I was stepping into the shower, kissed my cheek and hand, smiled, and turned away. Neither one of us dared look back. We were both developing an unhealthy attachment; I'd kill him if it got worse. Literally and figuratively. I leaned my head back under the running water, letting the heat all but burn my skin. I wanted it to wash away any feelings my heart had developed, but it didn't. Water wasn't enough to cleanse me. Of feelings or of my hobby.

Fifteen

AT THE OFFICE, I didn't say much to Julie. I was too deep in contemplation and trying to force out whatever that attachment to Devin was. Julie knew something was going on and also knew I'd talk when I was ready to. Instead, she came into my office with a list on the front of a piece of paper; times on the left side, names on the right. I didn't have to ask what this was. However, I was curious why she chose a simple handwritten list over the shared calendar. I accepted the paper and nodded.

"I'm okay, Jules. Don't worry."

"You know I'm here," she said as she turned and walked back into the reception area.

I went over the list, pulled my notepad out, and started writing out questions for each interview. At the top of each page, I wrote the interview's name, the time, and date. Each question was followed by a few blank lines for answers. This wasn't a form for the interviewee to fill out, but for me to fill out. I'd take notes or write a big, fat No under the question and cut the interview short. That was how I did things. It was how I landed Julie as an employee?

The time came for the first interview. She was on time, guided by Julie into my office. Julie sat next to her, across from my desk, so as not to seem opposing or even terrifying.

From my research into the criminals and other lowlifes my hobby forced me to deal with, as well as my extensive experience interviewing, literally, all kinds of people, I'd learned that interviews often made people who'd been locked up feel like they were sitting in front of a panel of prison officials, maybe a parole board, say, so this was a way to make them feel more at ease, this positioning of Julie.

For the interviewee, well, it put them more at ease. For me, of course—I was tempted to laugh maniacally when I thought about this—it was my way of flanking the candidate. Their attention would focus on me, giving my spy Julie the chance to size them up, to try to tease little details or giveaways out of their body language, tone of voice, eye movement, any blushing or sweat response, that kind of thing.

Of course, Julie, being the total pro she was, would also have her own list of questions, particularly for those who would be under her direct supervision or taking her seat in this office. Julie's approach was softer than mine, but she could be just as shrewd. Maybe that was one reason I subconsciously kept her so close.

We went through introductions and basic getting-to-know-each-other small talk, then slid into the questions. Today was the first interview for everyone on the schedule. We'd narrow down from here and had more first interviews scheduled throughout the rest of the week.

Julie and I carefully teamed up on every interviewee. By carefully, I mean that we didn't want to overwhelm anyone or scare them off or make them uncomfortable. Though we used the interviews to vet candidates, we'd both been on the interviewee side of the table before and hated the way we were made to feel like we were just another number in a long line of applicants. We tried the best we could to avoid that discomfort for our interviewees. Even though we only allotted thirty minutes per person, we were gentle and smooth. And I still got all the information about these people that I needed.

There were occasional hiccups when an interview would go off the rails. Most times it meant the person was a bit too excited for the interview. As a result of those nerves, they would slip up and say something inappropriate or reveal past unacceptable behavior toward coworkers. Those people were cut short and told they'd be contacted. We had a canned email response for them. It was sad—for them, really—but our time was precious, and we didn't want to waste theirs, either.

Job hunting sucked. Finding the right employee sucked harder. It wasn't fun for anyone involved.

Once lunchtime hit, we were annoyed. Not one of the five we had spoken with were even close to what we wanted. We ordered banh mi from the Vietnamese place down the street and discussed different approaches to the interviews scheduled for the afternoon. There was a lot of back and forth, ideas being tossed about, most ending in the garbage. Our sandwiches came, and we contemplated more ideas as we ate. Nothing seemed to be good enough or just right. We knew our current line of questioning was just right; we were just interviewing people who wouldn't fit.

It wasn't anything unusual, either. All employers went through this, no matter how carefully they prescreened. That is, unless they threw out vast amounts of applicants based on a paltry number of keywords. The federal government was notorious for that, claiming "streamline" when they only cared about who applicants were connected with. I may or may not have held a grudge there, knowing I shouldn't—that it was a blessing I didn't work for them.

If they hadn't shut me out more times than I could count, I wouldn't have Passing Through, and I sure as flies on shit would *not* have the ability to keep things to myself. Government coworkers were forever involved in each other's business. It was like a reality show set in high school and composed of grown adults. I used to see it a lot, less than enthused about the prospect.

Lunch ended, and we had a little bit of time before the next appointment. Julie and I went over the schedule for the rest of the week. Knowing we'd be lucky to pull five from this week into second interviews, we decided to keep the ads up. I'd also gotten an email from Kevin about possible office locations that I forwarded to Julie. She narrowed that list down to two. I laughed.

"Jules, really? Just two?"

"Well, you said I get input. And seriously, what the hell is wrong with Kevin? Nebraska by MLK," she giggled. "Only if I could have Applesauce protection-trained and bring him to the office."

"It is *not* that bad. Skeevy, yes. But not really violent. That's down by the dispatch center." We both cackled. Neither one of us was brought up with a lot of money, and I had friends who lived in the hood. Even they said it was bad yet still chose to live there. Some of them advised against Julie or me going there without them. Some places were just worse than others. Every city had its problems, Tampa included.

"How is Applesauce? Still eating the corner of the mattress, is he?"

"You shush about that." Julie tried not to laugh, but it was too funny. A mattress-eating dog. As in he actually swallowed what he bit off, except anything metal. He was the strangest dog ever. Even Minion wasn't that weird.

We were still laughing when our next appointment came through the door. He was tall with dark hair and bright blue eyes; the kind of guy I generally go for. I knew I had to write him off posthaste, but he was standing in front of Julie's desk, and I couldn't think of a way to tell him to kick rocks. I invited him back, and Julie drifted in behind him. She was making faces and close to drooling. I shot her a stern look, but of us trying to keep our cool.

I introduced myself, followed by Julie. We all shook hands and exchanged greetings. He said his name, but I didn't hear it. Hell, it was on both mine and Julie's notepads and the résumé on my desk. Neither one of us cared. I hoped he was oblivious and couldn't tell we had lost our abilities to speak. I restarted my brain first.

"I'm going to ask you the most hated interview question. Ready? Tell us about yourself."

He broke out into laughter. He told us about his love of hiking and climbing, that he had a Jeep for rock crawling, two cats, and a host of other things. I swear I fell in love in those forty-five seconds. Then it hit me. Like a sack of potatoes. He'd done his homework. No. This couldn't be real. FUCK!

"Are these things really your interests, or have you conducted some research?" I asked, one eyebrow raised.

"You got me." He hung his head only an inch. "I do enjoy hiking and rock climbing, but I don't have cats or a Jeep. I'm originally from Arizona. I didn't learn about all the fun Jeep things until I got here. But, yes, Ms. Cage, you're correct. I dug into your likes hoping it would help me get the job."

"Now that you say that, why do you want to work for me?"

Julie choked and turned red. She knew where I was going with this and, most likely, his response.

"Well, you're well connected."

Julie choked harder, turning a reddish-purple color.

"You're driven and ambitious."

Julie started to lean out of her chair.

"And you're a real bitch to work for, or so I'm told."

I looked at him, no readable expression on my face. I smiled. One that was too wide, too nice, too pretty. Julie straightened herself back in her chair. She looked at me, well aware of what was about to happen. I placed my hands on my desk, interlacing my fingers and making a steeple from both index fingers.

Julie pushed her chair back and stood up.

I leaned forward, eyes locked with Hot Guy.

"Get. Out. No more questions. Go. If you don't leave now, I'll be forced to protect myself and Julie against a trespasser. Goodbye." I motioned to a waiting Julie.

Hot guy looked at me, incredulous. His face flushed with embarrassment and maybe some anger. Whether that was at me or himself, I didn't care. He'd let his truth out and called me a bitch in the process. No one calls me that in an interview to work for me. He stood and turned to leave, not wanting to be arrested.

"Oh, one more thing," I called after him, "who referred you to me?"

Sixteen

JULIE TRIPPED OVER HER own feet, catching herself on my desk before she fell. I knew she was terrified by what might happen in the next thirty seconds.

"Stu Jones told me you were looking to open a new office."

I bit the end of my pen and shooed him away like a hog to slaughter. Wisely, he left.

Stu? Really? I picked up my phone, unable to remember what his current schedule was, and dialed. It rang three times before he answered.

"Hey, Brit!"

"Who the fuck did you send to me? That guy was a real douche."

"Oh shit. I didn't think he'd actually apply."

"Stu," the ire in my voice was enough to melt wallpaper glue, "spill it."

For the next three minutes, he told me Hot Guy was some rando he'd met at the gym. The guy worked for the city but was whining about his current job and how women ran the office and they were "catty twats" or something to that effect. Stu suggested he apply for one of my openings.

Dude then ran his own research on me, but we didn't know who told him I was "a real bitch to work for" since Julie was ever my only direct employee. Stu knew the guy had acquaintances on the force and promised he'd find out who. I wasn't sure I cared about the why aspect of their lies about me. It was probably someone who was friends with John Sweet and just mad about the whole situation. Because he probably considered me naive enough to fawn all over the guy who broke into my house.

"Whatever, man. Hot Guy the douche bag is gone. I told him if he didn't leave, I'd hit him with trespassing. He got the hint. A little mad maybe, but he'll get over it."

"Want me to come take a report?"

"Not you. Let's do this the official way and see who gets called out."

"You got it. And when are you free for lunch, B?"

"How does tomorrow sound?"

"Works for me. Anywhere special?"

"Grilled chicken and not fast food, I'm on a kick lately. The Pub? Cheesecake Factory? Some mom-and-pop joint? You pick."

"Why don't we just cook, then? I'll grill it and have it ready by the time you get here."

"Stu, that sounds too much like a date. I'm down to save money but that made me a little uncomfortable. Probably because you sent that douchey hot guy in here," I giggled.

He knew I was poking fun at his expense. He also knew he deserved it, even if just a little bit.

Stu laughed. "I got you, Brit. Fine. Noon at Moxie's."

"I'm there. Talk to you then."

Stu hung up before I did. I guessed he was more embarrassed about that guy than anything. I know I would be. I went back to work and enjoyed the rest of the day interviewing with Julie. There was a total of two more added to the list for second interviews, bringing the total to . . . two. There were more days in the week, thank God, and we'd already established we were keeping the ads up.

As for new office locations, Julie mentioned two whose locations she liked. She also said she gave Kevin shit for the list, but not if she wanted to go see them.

"Jules," I called as I started packing up for the day, "do you want to go look at those two offices in the morning? Our first appointment isn't until, like, eleven."

"I was thinking to drive and check them out now, but tomorrow sounds better. Both of us checking them out. Yeah, Brit, I like that. Meet here at nine?"

"Perfect. I'll drive us around. Be your *chauffeur*." We both laughed.

We always walked out together, hugging bye every day. It wasn't habit or routine, or maybe it was a little of both. We were friends, and this was what friends did.

On my drive home, something felt off. Like I was being followed. Me. Followed. *I'm* the one who follows people. I looked in my rearview mirror and didn't see anything. Left-side mirror was the same. Then I glanced in the right side mirror. There was a newer, navy-colored Honda swerving in and out of the right lane to get in behind me. I was driving the speed limit and not turning anytime soon, so I knew I was being followed. I looked again in the rearview, trying to see the driver, but the angle of the sun effectively prevented that.

It was fine, though. If whoever that was wanted to follow me in Tampa rush hour traffic, that was their own stupid move. I cut across two lanes of traffic, scaring the shit out of those I'd cut off, resulting in a chorus of honking. I couldn't figure out their issue, I had an inch to spare front and back to spare. The Honda couldn't follow, and I flipped them off as I made a right turn onto a side street.

I was driving along, amused by how terrible people were at driving these days, and then it happened.

The intersection didn't have a stop sign in my direction, but there was one on the cross street. That navy Honda blew through the stop sign and slammed into my heavily reinforced rear bumper and right at the quarter panel, scooting my Jeep to the side a little. I slammed on the brakes, shifted to park, and grabbed my KA-BAR. I stuck it in the back of my pants as I got out. Angry couldn't begin to describe what was going on inside me.

I heard sirens and neighbors came running out asking if anyone was hurt. One of them had a cell phone to their ear, likely on the phone with dispatch, who told them to stay on the line until help arrived.

Ignoring the helpful people, I lumbered toward the Honda. The front- and side-impact airbags on the driver side had deployed. I expected that. I also expected the driver to be dazed, at the absolute least. The door was open, a leg dangling out. No blood or anything like you'd see in a movie. Just a leg of a person—regretfully—still alive.

"Hey, man. Did you *not* see the stop sign?"

"Ugh, no," he groaned. He was full of shit. He was following me, and I wanted to know who he was and why. I couldn't see his face because it was still buried in the airbags. Better for him, I suppose. I thought about ripping the airbags with my KA-BAR but knew better. If he really was injured, I didn't need people seeing me make it worse. But how I'd have loved to "accidentally" slice his pretty face.

I had a suspicion it was douchey-hot guy from earlier, and the shoe looked like the ones he had on. So I asked him.

"Do you know me?"

"Stop, lady. My head hurts."

"You're full of shit, pal. I saw you follow me until I thought I lost you. You hit me on purpose. Who are you, and why are you following me?" The more heated I got, the meaner I sounded.

"Fine, fine," he sighed, "yes, I interviewed with you earlier. I wanted to scare you for kicking me out."

I laughed like I did when I daydreamed about cutting people open. "Well, I guess you fucked that right up, huh? In case you didn't already know, the job isn't yours. I'll also make sure your superiors know about this. You did this to yourself."

As soon as I'd finished speaking, a police car came rolling up, sirens close behind. Stu got out of the patrol car. I didn't think this could get any funnier. Then I looked at my bumper. Stu ran over and started questioning me like he's supposed to, also stopping me from gutting the fish behind the wheel of the trashed Honda. I wanted to move Stu from in front of my face, but I knew better. He tried to calm me down. I tried myself. None of it was making me feel any less violent.

Then Stu asked if I knew the guy.

"You do, too."

"Oh? Ohhhhhhh. No. Please no."

"Yes," I motioned to the Honda, "go see for yourself. I mean, it's your job."

"That was cold, Brit."

"I've never been accused otherwise." I smirked as he walked to the Honda. I wanted Stu, and I was on the verge of falling for Devin. This was horrible. I'd found myself in a sticky situation, all puns intended.

Seventeen

Stu pulled some lame story from Douche Guy. Something about how he wasn't paying attention. Stu called him out on that lie, and he caved. He admitted he followed me in an attempt to scare me but swore he was sorry he hit my Jeep. We all knew that was bullshit. What he was really sorry about was that we were pressing every charge we could get to stick. Stalking, reckless driving, the works. Stu even filed for a restraining order on my behalf.

He didn't need to do that. I could've handled it. But I understood his protection of me. I'd already been almost fucked over by one of his former coworkers and now this. Stu was a good friend, and it sucked we felt the way we did about each other. It *had* to be this way. I didn't want to kill him; I would if I had to.

Douche Guy was cuffed to a gurney and transported via ambulance to the hospital for evaluation. I was fine. Pissed off to an immeasurable level but physically fine. Stu urged me to get checked out. So I had him follow me home to drop off my Jeep, and he drove me to the ER.

The drive was awkward. He kept trying to apologize, and I kept telling him to stop feeling bad.

"Look, shit happens. We meet great people; we meet shitty people. You're a good guy, Stu. Please stop beating yourself up over this. You didn't tell him to react the way he did. That's on him."

He glanced at me in the rearview. "I know but I still feel bad."

"If I wasn't stuck in this back hellhole, I'd slap you. Stop. Stu, there's nothing to forgive you for."

He did stop talking. He looked in the mirror again, and I could see he was trying to process and accept what I'd said.

We arrived at the hospital not long after. The docs checked me out, wrote me a script for 800 milligrams of ibuprofen and let me go. I didn't plan to fill it, but, again, Stu insisted. He also insisted on staying with me that night. I wanted to tell him no, but I didn't have the heart to. This was his way of trying to make everything better. Not for me. For his own conscience.

His shift ended at eight, and he picked up Thai on his way to my house. Like those of us who frequent gyms, he had a go bag with clean clothes and hygiene essentials. We ate at the coffee table then took turns showering. He said he wanted to be available if I conked out. Whatever. I get he felt bad, but I was feeling like the patient of an overbearing doctor or nurse.

"Stu, my dear, sweet Stu. You're killing me with all this care." If I pleaded any more, and with those sad dog eyes, he'd break. Like, physically break.

"Brit, I screwed up. If it wasn't for me—"

"STOP. It happened and it's done. I appreciate your help, I truly do, but you're suffocating me. Back up. Just a little. Please."

"I'm sorry. I didn't mean to upset you. Man, I can't do any-thing right these days. Just my job." He hung his head, a tear falling from his eye closest to me.

I reached around and hugged him. We sat that way for what seemed like forever. It was about twenty minutes. I pulled back, intending to stand up. As I did, Stu pulled my arm, causing me to fall back down onto the couch. I wanted what he wanted. But I had to resist. My bitch side was about to come out to play, and I stopped her.

"Stu—" Tears stung my eyes. "I can't. I love you so much, but we can't be together. I'm not right for you. I'm selfish and, quite honestly, a huge villain. I hate that I have to say this at all. I wish things could be different. You deserve better than me."

I kissed his wet cheek. "If you're not here when I'm finished my shower, I'll understand and respect that."

Once in the shower, I cried so hard I was sure there were more tears down the drain than gallons of water. All I could hear in my head was the song by Hinder "Better Than Me."

I think you can do much better than me
After all the lies that I made you believe…

I felt like dog shit set on fire and stomped out on someone's doorstep. Who I was wasn't fair to anyone who loved or cared about me, even in the smallest amounts. I killed people. I was a monster, and I didn't know why, other than I was born this way. And I enjoyed it. I enjoyed the stalk, the planning, the killing. Even when it was dull and boring and exhausting. The high that came from the kill, from watching the light go out in someone's eyes…There was no other way to replicate that without illicit drugs—and even then, drugs ran a distant second.

I didn't expect what I saw when I went back downstairs. Stu, sitting on the couch, Minion on his lap. I fought the onslaught of feelings until they bled out from every pore. I sank to the floor as soundless as possible, but Minion knew I was there. That alerted Stu. He picked me up off the floor and set me on the couch across from him, covering me with the throw I had on the back. Then, struggling himself, Stu went to the guest room to shower and change.

I don't know how long he was gone for. All I remember was crying myself to sleep. I woke up to the TV on and Stu flicking through channels, stealing glances at me. I rubbed my eyes as I sat up. They were swollen and sore. I met Stu's puffy, red-eyed gaze and half smiled. I moved over and sat next to him, dropping my head onto his shoulder. He put his arm around me and kissed my forehead.

"Britney, I adore you, and I always will. I respect you and your decisions, and yeah, it is crazy that I have such strong feelings for you after knowing for such a short time. I still want to be your friend. If it gets too hard, I'll let you know. Can you do the same for me?"

I nodded, more tears trickling. Stu handed me what was left of the box of tissues. I laughed.

"I only keep one box out because a three-pack lasts me more than the average person. I'll grab another." I shifted and tried to stand. Stu gave me a look that said he would get them if I told him where they were.

"The guest room closet. Top shelf."

Stu stood, handing me the remote as he did, and walked out of the room. I wanted my bed, but I also wanted to stay by his side on the couch. So I flicked through the live streaming channels and found nothing. I decided to put the *Hannibal* TV series on. It felt fitting. Stu came back, new box of tissues in hand, and sat. We watched and felt the raw emotions on screen as well as on our own.

Then the sun was up. We'd fallen asleep sitting up on the couch, me curled in his arm. I felt worse than last night, though now it was more physical. I searched the coffee table for my phone and couldn't find it. My movements woke Stu.

"Sorry. Didn't mean to wake you," came my hoarse apology.

"It's okay. I think I'm right on time to call out." He gave a halfhearted chuckle.

"That's why I'm trying to find my phone." I stood and went to my purse hanging on the pegs by the door. After a minute or so of digging around, I pulled it out. Over thirty missed messages—texts and calls combined. Stu had, at some point last night, called Julie and told her. She then told the girls. I sighed. The bigger issue being that I wasn't going into the office today. Nor were Julie and I going to look at those two potential offices.

I responded in the group text that I was okay and made a joke about this stalker not being the guy I'm sleeping with. The girls didn't think it was funny.

Then I called Julie. We talked for a few minutes, and she offered to go look at the offices just her and Kevin, but I wasn't having it. We'd agreed to go together, and that was still the plan. Jules sounded relieved that I was still my stubborn self. We hung up so she could reschedule the day's interviews.

Stu was just walking back out into the living room as I hung up.

"Okay, I'm good for the day. Paid too. Now, would you like some coffee and breakfast?"

"Does a fish swim? But I have a special request."

"Well, you are the one who was stalked—again—so I think a special request is allowed." Stu sounded jovial, but his eyes said different.

"I could really go for a true Jewish Reuben. Yes, for breakfast."

Stu smiled so wide, knowing I was somewhat back to myself. Then he used his phone to order from one of the delivery apps while I went to make coffee. He didn't try to stop me, and for that I was grateful. I waited for the coffee to finish, staring out the patio door, lost in my thoughts. We'd be all right, Stu and I. We'd stay friends and still have the feelings we did. Maybe one of us would get over them, but the other wouldn't. That's how these things went. I'd been there a few too many times. One of them was forever in my heart. I'd rather not talk about him. Ever. It had been years, and it still hurt.

I poured us both coffee as the doorbell rang. Glorious food had arrived.

Eighteen

RIGHT ALONG WITH THAT glorious food was a gaggle of reporters. There was nothing sacred to these people. I found myself—again—the hot topic of the day. At least it wasn't for shooting a cop this time. Though there was a cop taking the food from the delivery person. I was the best and worst news topic ever. I laughed out loud and waved. Stu closed the door.

"What is wrong with them?" His face turned a shade of red I hadn't seen before.

"Well, I was stalked and crashed into, but still, this is a big city. Must really be a slow news day if they're hassling me. You at the door definitely makes things more…interesting." I nudged him in the ribs, and we laughed. "Let's play with them and see where it goes."

"Brit, I couldn't."

I let out a heavy breath. "You're right. I can't either. It'll mess with us more than them. I'm sorry. I didn't mean to hurt you."

"Shush. We've got a great breakfast here, and I smell that coffee. Let's eat. If we want to spend the rest of the day together, cool. If not, I'll go home." He smiled at me as he set the bag of food down.

We ate and laughed at the reporters trying to sneak photos. My lawyer called and said he'd release a statement. I told him I'd hold a press conference outside my front door in an hour. Apparently, the local affiliate was spending a week on violence against women, and my personal tragedy dovetailed nicely into the day's news package. And because TV reporters suffered from a herd mentality, all the other local stations had caught wind and shown up, too.

The lawyer disagreed about my doing the presser alone—being a typical lawyer, he wanted input on anything I'd say to the cameras and wanted to be there to bail me out when one of the local reporters invariably threw out what they thought would be a gotcha question—but hung up to make the necessary calls.

Osten was having a conniption of his own. He hadn't heard from me in a couple weeks and now this. To compound his worry, I wasn't responding to his texts or calls.

After I finished my breakfast, I called him back. He admonished me like I was a child. I deserved it. He was so worried about me that his blood pressure was up and that was reason enough for his home nurse to try to convince him to go to the hospital. Everything was a mess. Because of me. This was why I kept a small circle. And it still got fucked up.

I felt like a letdown for scaring Joe so bad. Apologies only got anyone so far. I tried to calm him down, but I also knew that only time would do that.

"Joe, I'm doing a press conference outside my house in about a half an hour. In my pajamas. I'm fine, and you'll be able to see for yourself. No cuts or scrapes, but my rear bumper was scratched. That's part of why it was so armored. Please, watch and see. I love you, Dad t=Two."

"Fiiiine, I'll watch. But don't think you're in the clear with me, Missy."

"Joe. Really? I'm okay and you know it. Now who's the child?"

He laughed, a hearty one. He was much more relaxed than when he first answered the phone. "Brit, come for dinner tonight."

"How about tomorrow? I intend to hang around the house in my pajamas all day, in and out of naps like Minion."

"I'm holding you to it."

"I'll bring wine. I love you, Joe. And I appreciate you more than I'll ever be able to express."

"Love you too, Brit."

Thinking about dads, I should probably have called my father. Then I thought better of it. He was at work. It was a Friday morning. Then again, he never did tell me when he was taking random days off. I sent him a text to see what he was doing.

Working. You okay?

Yeah, great. Call me when you get home?

Sure. Love you.

Love you too, Pops.

That was that. Now I needed to brush my teeth and floss the sauerkraut from between some of them. And my breath was rank. I didn't bother freshening my face up. I wanted the city, and whoever else would be watching, to see me as vulnerable. To think I wasn't immune to crazy. I also wanted them to know that no matter what I went through, I was abso-fucking-lutely NOT a victim.

Stu was at the bottom of the stairs in a show of support. I hugged him, took a steadying breath, opened the door, and stepped out into the crowd of reporters gathered on my walkway. I hated being on live TV. This was unfortunate, but it needed to be done. I didn't want other women think-ing they needed to play the part of victim when they were stronger than that. Mostly, I was challenging any would-be stalkers and dumbasses. *Come for me, and watch what happens to you.*

All the reporters asked the same questions, worded differently. They were lazy and lacked creativity. One asked why I thought this kept happening to me.

"Because I attract crazy," I laughed, and the reporters joined in. I thanked them for their time and went back in the house.

Stu laughed. "Really, Brit? Because I attract crazy?"

"Well, you're still here."

We laughed and sat back down on the couch. We wasted the rest of the day until my dad called. He'd seen the press conference and was a little less than happy that I didn't tell him that it was something important I wanted to talk to him about it, but I didn't think it was as big a deal as everyone made it out to be.

Then his tone changed to something along the lines of scolding. He launched into a rant about how I was so flippant about my own safety. I had to remind him that I carried and had no qualms shooting anyone in self-defense. Then I reminded him that I shot the cop who broke into my house. He apologized, though he admitted he still believed I was outwardly too careless. He didn't understand. I wanted people to believe that, including him. I told him what he wanted to hear and hung up.

Stu looked at me, curious but cool. He didn't ask, either. He knew I lived my life the way I wanted to, and no amount of protective care would stop me. But he did make an observation. One I found bothersome.

"He's right, you know."

I cringed. "You're all entitled to your own opinions."

Stu left after dinner but not before loading the dishwasher for me and starting it. He really was a good friend and—nope, had to get those thoughts out of my head. Right then.

I felt better when I woke up to the sun barely peeking through the clouds. I felt like I could get back to my routine and go for a jog. And that's what I did. I started out slower than usual, though. My head was a little swimmy with the exertion, as the ER doctor warned might happen. I kept the slow pace, which was more like a brisk walk. I tried to clear my head of all that had taken place the past two days. I was able to push the comments about my safety aside, but the feelings for Stu kept creeping back up. There was maybe another way to handle that.

No, no there wasn't. Devin and I had decided to take a break because we were getting too used to each other and wanted to really get to know each other and all that crap.

"FUCK!"

Those in earshot searched for where the shout came from or were close enough to know and looked dead at me. I forgot how loud I could get. This was a disaster. I needed to get back to the sisters, Jimin and Suk, anyway. On them, I could focus. I still had more hours to watch them at home and eventually follow their rides. Given they were sort of freelancers and tax deadlines loomed, following their rides during normal work hours would be useless. April 16th, I'd make my move. That was only a few weeks away.

Not only did I have to learn their routines; I had to go to Gainesville and scope out the place this would all go down. I wasn't looking forward to the drive, but I'd do it on a week-end.

And I needed to have my Jeep checked out to make sure the bumper didn't need replacing or any other work done. I called the shop on the walk back home, and they told me to come by in an hour. One thing off the list of things to do.

After I got back and cleaned up, I called Julie.

"Hey. I'm sorry for being short yesterday. Do you want to go look at those two offices tomorrow?"

"Brit, there's no need to apologize. I'm sure you were slammed with texts and calls and emails. And yes, that sounds great. I can share some more adoption news with you face to face."

My heart sank, but Julie didn't sound sad. In fact, she sounded like she was trying to hide excitement.

"Is everything okay?"

"More than I can say right now. I'll come to your house in the morning, and I'll call Kevin now." Julie had to hang up; she couldn't contain the words that wanted to come out.

"Okay. See you then."

Now I was excited. So many questions ran through my head, wondering if they'd met a child they fell in love with, or maybe the child already lived with them. The possibilities were almost endless. My favorite part was that Julie wasn't sad or down. Tomorrow would be amazing, for sure. Today would be awkward.

The guys at the shop pulled the bumper and inspected everything. They even put my Jeep on the lift to check the suspension, since the hit slid me a little. I knew I wasn't allowed in the shop, so I leaned against the frame of the garage door. I enjoyed watching them work. I'd always wanted to do things to my Jeep myself, but it was more effective and safer to have professionals handle it.

They were finished a few minutes shy of an hour after starting. All was well with my Jeep, just a few scratches they offered to touch up for me. I promised to make an appointment and thanked them for taking care of me so well.

I had a few hours to kill before going to Joe's for dinner, so I did the usual keeping up-around-the-house stuff. That took all of twenty minutes. Time for research. I grabbed my laptop and started looking at the place in Gainesville I was going to use as my kill and disposal site. Their hours weren't my concern; they closed fairly early.

The problem was that it was on a college campus—a sprawling one with its own police force and surveillance cameras everywhere, not to mention what I was sure were their top-notch alarm systems. I'd have to have a look-see and maybe a tour before I could have a proper plan.

I had a hacker friend who worked at SOCOM—sorry, I meant US Special Operations Command, the headquarters for all American Special Forces activity across the world at any given time. This guy was more connected than a power station. I called him and asked for a favor I didn't quite know the details of yet. He said yes and to call him when I had the rest of what I needed.

Now it was closer to the time I needed to head over to Joe's, so I did just that. He was so happy to see me, I think he cracked a rib hugging me. Or maybe it would just be bruised; it hurt but was worth it. He started to yell at me again, but I stopped him with a smile. That was all it took. He saw me smile and knew I was okay.

We sat at the bar/island in the kitchen. He poured me a glass of merlot and even had one himself. I didn't want to mom him, so I let it go. He was paying a nurse to live there and tell him what he could and couldn't do. Who was I to tell him one wasn't allowed? We didn't speak for a few minutes, simply enjoying each other's company and the wine. Joe set his glass down and looked at me. *Really* looked at me.

"You look good for someone who's been stalked twice now."

"Am I supposed to look bad?"

"Well, dear, I am a plastic surgeon, and I see victims all the time."

I got loud in a hurry.

Nineteen

I CRACKED MY NECK, set my glass down as carefully as I could, and, as calmly as I could, pointedly explained that the victims he worked with were survivors of disease. I didn't believe in victimhood for the sake of being a victim. True victims were those struck by disease or those who chose to give up or couldn't fight anymore; true victims were innocents preyed upon by those who knew better. The only patients of Joe's who actually were victims were those tortured by themselves and society, pressured to look different than how they did. Hell, I was sometimes victimized by my own mind and feelings; I thought about plastic surgery to fix what society said wasn't appealing about me.

Joe Osten was rarely disagreed with, let alone the way I just had. He simply sat there and let me get all that off my chest, sounding mean and degrading toward him. He looked at me and smiled. *Not* the reaction I expected but was grateful for. He wasn't getting mad or upset. He was genuinely trying to see from my perspective. I hugged him without a word. I could've told him I was proud of him, but knowing him the way I do, this moment wasn't the right one.

"Britney, I admire you. You stick to your convictions and are one of the strongest women I know. I'm so proud of you."

There was my chance. "I'm proud of you, too, Joe. You kept calm and tried to see from where I stand. And thank you. Your love and respect mean everything to me."

Joe stood, wine in hand, and handed me my glass. He walked over to the table, nodding for me to join him so we could finish our conversation over dinner.

The food was takeout on plates from my favorite Indian restaurant. The conversation was almost as good as the food, though food was preferable to anything for me. I was feeling much less swimmy too, which was great. Joe and I had a genuinely relaxing evening. It was the first I could remember in a long time. We'd both grown so much, especially in our businesses, that we really didn't relax often.

Joe mentioned something about going outside for a cigar. I glared at him, and he laughed from his belly.

"I was kidding. Like you, I said it for the reaction."

I smirked. "You know too much about me. I have to kill you now."

We clinked glasses and sipped. I had missed this. But it wasn't like either of us could do this weekly anymore. Me because, well, I killed people. And when I wasn't killing them, I was stalking them and planning ways to kill them.

And Joe had to take it easier because he had to keep his stress levels down, even with the meds he was on. I was satisfied with monthly dinners.

I wasn't allowed to help clean up. My hands were slapped away by the housekeeper. She laughed, as always, at my trying to help. It was her job, and she enjoyed it; Joe was good to his people. Like anyone, he could be a stubborn shit sometimes too. Overall, he was a good man who valued and appreciated those who worked for him. He got nosey about Alex, and I told him I hadn't heard a word. I mean, how could I? The kid was dead by my hand.

The night came to a close, and I hugged Joe goodbye, thanking him for being him and for dinner.

By the time I got home, all I wanted to do was sleep. But when I got to my driveway, I saw a familiar car parked outside my house. Devin's car. Not that I wasn't excited by the prospect of amazing sex. I was more irritated that he had just shown up unannounced. Maybe I had to tell him how well that didn't go over with me. I parked in my garage as Devin exited his car. I waited for him, and we walked inside together.

After we saw stars, I explained that I didn't do unannounced visits, regardless how good the sex was. He apologized and offered to make it up to me. I was contemplating asking how, and then my body found out.

I fell asleep on his chest, with my alarm set. Julie would be by in the morning, and I had some explaining to do.

Devin shot me a dirty look when the alarm went off. One that I felt like giving myself. But Julie would be here in about an hour, and I wanted to be ready when she got here. Preferably with him gone.

"Look, Julie's gonna be here in an hour so we can go look at new locations for Passing Through. Well, a second office. Anyway, I don't think you should be here when she shows up. Unless you want to explain that we're sleeping together and nothing more?"

"Nope. Thanks, though," he laughed and rolled out of bed. He got dressed as I showered, and he wouldn't leave until I was out so I could lock the door.

I really wished people would stop treating me like glass. I already broke, and the only one who knew it was Stu and that was a different break. If someone broke into the house again, I'd be pissed to have to clean up more blood. I didn't say anything about it to Devin. He was bothered enough by our attachment to each other, almost as much as I was. I needed to stop worrying about men, though. I had priorities, and they weren't on that list.

Julie had a key and let herself in, carrying two hot coffee concoctions. One was a peppermint mocha for me, and hers was a caramel macchiato. I was just coming down the stairs to feed Minion when she walked in. It was good that she noticed me, or we would have collided, and that would've been an abuse of caffeine. She laughed and followed me to the kitchen.

"Spill," I said, sitting at the table after feeding an unhappy cat.

"Whatever you said to Maria—the social worker?—made her fall even more in love with us wanting to adopt. We're going to meet a bunch of kids next weekend, and it's a huge thanks to you. We owe you."

"You owe me shit." I stood and hugged her so tight. I was genuinely happy for her and Cody. I wanted them to be the happiest people on the planet. I'd do whatever I had to make sure they were.

I sipped my drink and started for the garage. "Let's go look at these places, shall we?"

Julie followed.

By the time we got back to my house, we couldn't stop laughing. The offices were far too absurd for us to even be mad at Kevin about them. The first one had peeling paint and ridiculous wallpaper. And the second one wasn't bad except it had wall-unit air-conditioning and was exorbitantly priced. I needed the laughter this morning brought. It'd been a rough few days. Several notes were made in an email to Kevin, along with a heartfelt thanks for making us laugh so hard.

He seemed hurt when he called after reading said email but understood why we found it funny. He'd seen the press conference and genuinely felt bad this kept happening. I told him, like I'd told everyone else, I was just glad it wasn't another cop. He agreed to keep looking for us and screen them more carefully.

Julie offered to stay with me, but I told her it was unnecessary. She was hesitant, but she went home.

I changed and hopped back into my Jeep, Gainesville bound.

Twenty

INTERSTATE 75 WAS A disaster south of Tampa, but it wasn't totally awful headed north. There was a lot of construction, but nothing like I-275 back in town. In this state, major highways and interstates were *always* under construction because the weather was nice enough. The problem was how long it took to get anything done at all.

I found my way off 75 to the campus and drove around. I wasn't putting the address in my GPS, even though I knew my location was always being tracked. I only cared if I got caught. Besides, I had friends up here. And touristy things I could do. Those were really lame excuses, but hey, I've yet to be suspected by anyone other than cops who break into my house.

I tooted around aimlessly, like a tourist, until I managed to find the facility. It was an unassuming building situated on a large lot between two brick buildings I could only believe were class-related labs and classrooms. The research I'd done said they were only open to the public on Fridays. Today was Sunday. I hung around the parking lot, inside my Jeep, for about an hour before deciding to get out and check out the building itself. No security came around in that hour, so I figured it safe enough to pull a baseball cap over my head, bill down and head down as I walked.

I circled the building, checking for cameras and entrances. There were keypads and swipe-card readers. All of these were easily hacked. The cameras were a different situation. They were on every corner, each with a 360 view. They also appeared to have night vision. It was a college, why would they skimp? Then I remembered my college campus and how lacking they were compared to this one. I was almost now ashamed to admit where I went. But my school had one of the top business schools in the country, so I guess that evened things out. That was a lie. Whatever. I'd have to come back and try to spend a full weekend here, even get in during their public hours. It would take a few days to get a swipe card anyhow.

I walked back to my Jeep, still not seeing security, police, or anyone. This area was somehow dead. I wasn't complaining. I had work to do here with two very unlucky philistines. Sucked to be them.

The drive home seemed faster than the drive up, like any other road trip did. It was dark, and the streetlights had been on for hours when I got home. I even waved to the nosey old bat looking out through her blinds. Fuck her. She had nothing else to do but be up in everyone's business. I'd target her, but she was too well known in this community. Not that I'd be suspect number one, but I lived across the street from her, and the cops would find it hard to believe I didn't see or hear anything. Especially given my track record the past year.

Stalkers needed to be smarter. Mine were far from that. I've made mistakes—hell, I was currently making them—but not enough to get caught like John Sweet and Douche Guy. I laughed. Their idiocy was amusing. I hadn't made mistakes that large, though I'd surely allowed large distractions. I put a stop to that a couple days ago, though. Stu and I were working on dealing with our feelings, and I was finding it easier to distance myself from Devin, with the obvious exception of sex.

Now that I'd have time and no one to worry about showing up uninvited, I could put my focus where it belonged: Julie and Cody's adoption, finding a second office, and taking down Jimin and Suk.

Monday morning brought an anticipated, but seriously underestimated, shitstorm. There were people lined up at the office door. Julie had locked herself inside. When I reached the door, I turned and looked at the line. Their faces wore concerned looks—was it for me, having seen the news? But they were desperate enough to be here for a job, which told me, in no uncertain terms, they didn't actually care. Little did they realize, I didn't either.

"We'll be with you shortly," I said so the whole line could hear. "If you're here to apply for a placement, stay in line. If you're here for anything else, you can leave unless you're scheduled to be here now."

There was a low grumble, followed by "What if we're here to apply for a direct opening?"

Moron. "You can leave. The ads specifically state no calls or visitors will be accepted."

"Well, that's fucked up."

I stalked down the line, looking for this tool. I found him and stuck my hand out to shake.

"I'm Britney. You are?"

"Uh, shit, I, um. Sorry." He took off to a car I couldn't see, a wet spot on his pants. Was I that scary? Maybe I was since I'd taken down two of my own stalkers now. I wasn't sure, but as I walked back to Julie waiting at the door, the line dispersed. There were five left standing.

I nodded for Julie to unlock the door. There was more than enough room for those five people to sit inside and fill out applications. Once inside, I asked those here for temp jobs to sit at one of the computers. That was three people. The other two were our first two interviews of the day. I respect "You're on time if you're early, but if you're on time, you're late" or however the saying went; I lived my life by that most of the time. But to be an entire thirty minutes early? Wait in the car for fifteen minutes, damn.

As I walked into my office, Julie asked the interviewees to take a seat and we'd be with them in turn. She scrambled after me, notepad clutched to her chest. I wasn't angry; I was annoyed by how many people couldn't follow simple directions. I'm sure they came to see "The Crazy Flame," as the media now called me. I mean really. Couldn't they have come up with something different? There were comic book characters with better names, for fuck's sake.

"Jules, I'm not mad. You did what you could. Really. It's cool. Let me get situated, and we can call the first one in. While I do that, do you mind getting the applicants started on the computers?"

"Not at all, Brit," she heaved out a breath. "I won't lie; I thought you might explode."

I laughed, "Nah. They're just dumb and desperate. And they probably wanted to see if I looked broken or something. I'm now a sideshow freak on top of everything else."

We both laughed, and Julie went to help those on the computers. I settled down at my desk and pulled my notepad and the résumés of the two scheduled back-to-back. They were both rather impressive on paper. It was time to talk to them.

I called for Julie, and she knew to bring the first one back.

A dark-haired woman, approximately thirty-four or so, dressed in a black suit with a green top that set off her dark gray eyes, and black flats. I cringed; I couldn't do flats because I felt the ground, and that hurt my feet. She introduced herself to both of us and shook our hands. Firm handshake; I liked that. Her name was Barbra.

"Barbra, was it? Please, sit." I sat, indicating I wasn't the stuffy person people thought I was.

"Please, call me Barb."

"No problem. Barb, why did you apply to be the office assistant? I see here you're more than qualified to run the office. And please don't think of this as a regular interview. I want you to be as relaxed as possible." Not that I was. I was champing at the bait dangling in front of my killer side . I could have easily made up a lie to go after that dick who pissed his pants outside…

"I can be honest, and you won't hold it against me?" She was skeptical, naturally. No one is ever honest in an interview; we all have to put on a show and a phony personality until we've worked somewhere long enough to show even a sliver of ourselves.

"You can."

"I don't want the responsibility."

Julie looked at me and nodded. We both had an appreciation for Barb right now. That she could be this honest, I was tempted to hire her immediately. Julie had an important question, however. "How do you feel about working for someone a few years younger than you?"

Barb looked at both of us, trying to guess our ages before she responded.

"I'm totally okay with it. You're not teenagers, and together you two have earned quite the reputation in high circles. I can only hope I'd do you justice."

Jules and I looked at each other and smiled.

"Barb, I'm not asking you back for a second interview."

Her face drooped.

"I'd like to bring you on. Or, if you're more comfortable giving us a try for a week or so, you can do that," I offered with a smiled.

"Really? You mean it? Oh wow! I'd love to take the try-out option, if I may," Barb beamed. She was so formal, so polite.

"We'll email you the contract today then," Julie said.

We all stood and shook hands. Barb thanked us too many times to count and left. I went to check on the applicants at the computers. Two were still typing away, and one was finished. I asked if he could leave me his name and handed him a sticky note. He scribbled something and smiled. I accepted it and told him we'd be in touch. I did the same for the other two women still working. I didn't want to ask them to wait to be interviewed for placement and waste half their day. I liked to think I was a little more considerate than that. They happily obliged, grateful that I respected their time.

I motioned for the man waiting for his interview. He had applied for the manager spot. I already decided I wasn't hiring him, but his résumé was fairly impressive, and if I wasn't hiring him, I was sure I'd know someone who could.

Once we were seated, he cleared his throat and spoke. "I'm James, Jim for short. I'd like to be honest and tell you I'm actually not interested in working for you."

"Well, Jim, thanks. In equal honesty, I don't want to hire you. But I am nothing short of a stunning hiring manager.

That said, I chose to bring you in because you have an out-standing résumé. You've been around and, forgive my bluntness, don't look a day over twenty-six."

"I am," he responded, "twenty-six, I mean."

"Damn, I'm good." We all laughed, and Julie looked at me like I had three heads. I went back to Jim.

"So, Jim. What do you want to do?"

"I'd like to be an officer or CFO somewhere important. Maybe with one of the law firms you work with?"

"Jim, I do think your résumé fits. I'll tell you what. Let me make some calls, and I'll get back to you. I won't make promises, but let me see what I can find out. Sound good?"

He nodded. "Yes, thank you very much, Ms. Cage."

We shook hands, and Julie walked him to the door.

Twenty-One

JULIE CAME BACK INTO my office, looking at me like I'd just spoken Latin out of nowhere.

"What?"

"How did you know? *Both of them*. I mean, that was unreal."

"I studied human resources, Jules. I've studied human behavior, for many years. I can read people. It's actually kind of sickening. How many more do we have today?"

"Two after lunch."

"Awesome. I'll have time to make the calls and go over the three temps who applied today."

"I'll go over them; you handle the Jim thing."

"The Jim thing?" I asked, half laughing.

"You know what I meant." She tore off a page, crumpled it, and threw it at me.

"Yeah, yeah. Get back to work," I smirked.

And we did just that. I called two lawyers before calling the top in the city. No surprise; his name was Jim also. And he represented me. He said to bring the guy in for a real interview and if I liked him enough, he'd call him for another. I agreed and called applicant Jim as soon as I hung up with Lawyer Jim. Applicant Jim said he could come back tomorrow at ten. That worked for me, so I scheduled him.

I searched my computer for the contract to send to Barb, stating that she was agreeing to work for me for a week to see if she liked it enough to stay and that her only obligation was to inform me, either way, in writing. There was an hourly pay rate on there as well, which was more than fair given her work record. I signed and emailed it to her. That seemed to take care of the immediate.

Now I was onto the three temp applicants. Julie forwarded me two, knowing we couldn't place one of the women due to time constraints. Julie sent her one of the canned emails that stated we didn't have anything for her at the moment, but she should keep us informed of her availability if she wanted to.

The other woman didn't answer, so I left her a voicemail. The young man, however, answered on the first ring.

"This is Julius." His tone was upbeat.

"Hey, Julius, it's Britney Cage from Passing Through Temp Agency. Do you have a few minutes?"

"I do."

"Great," I said and launched into my questions that pertained to what he wanted to do. Within ten minutes, I had him placed with a local printing company. Julius was a graphic designer, and this company had a hard time keeping good people because the owner wasn't the easiest person to work for. Or that's what my temps kept telling me when they asked for new assignments. Which was why I always seemed to have an opening for a graphic designer.

Julius seemed like a nice enough guy, just down on his luck. He was transparent enough to inform me that he would be looking for permanent work while temping and asked if I came across anything to let him know. I agreed. I didn't want anyone I placed to hate their placement, and therefore me, for placing them there. Passing Through wasn't just about placing quality temps in quality work; it was about helping people grow and becoming the best they could be at what they did.

Julius agreed to start in two days. The company just lost another employee and was slammed with work. Julius wouldn't be difficult to train, given he knew all the software they used. He was quite gifted at what he did. If I needed a new logo, I'd probably call him first.

All that done, I was able to call my SOCOM friend about a key card to get me into the slaughterhouse/packing facility. He said I'd have it by the end of the week. He also said something about being able to disable the cameras. I wasn't asking. He said he'd handle it remotely. I still hated needing help for any of this, but when it came to high tech, I was high stupid. Maybe one day I'd try to learn, but I also knew that was a level of expertise I didn't possess. Nor a level of patience. Regardless how much time I'd spent in China and practicing patience—even pursuing it—I knew in my bones that hacking and tech weren't mine to understand.

The best part about having friends in such high places was that they made sure our conversations never happened. Even if we were catching up over coffee, they could erase any record of those meetings. If I ever wanted to disappear proper, this guy had ties to those who could help make that happen. As it stood, I enjoyed my life. Stalkers and all.

Lunch had come and gone, and I'd gotten Julius' paperwork back. I was still waiting on Barb's signed contract, but I knew I'd have it by the end of the day. I'd add more days depending on when she got it back to me, so that wasn't an issue. In the interim, I'd get Julius squared away.

Oh, the tedium. It was a love-hate relationship, but I really enjoyed the majority of the work. Julie was still sifting through potential applicants for another assistant. She pulled the ads for hiring manager because she'd decided she was going to try it. If she wanted to come back, she'd hire someone to take her place. Not a big thing. To her it was. I had no worries. I trusted her implicitly.

Around three, I received an email from Barb. She wanted to know if she could start next Monday instead of this week, something about she wanted to be in top shape or something. Whatever that meant, I was fine with it. I amended the contract and sent it back. Almost immediately, she signed and returned it. Sweet. Now we'd have an assistant to train. Whether Barb would stay was on her. Though I was sure it would be more of a question of whom she stayed with.

Julie messaged me through our system, telling me that Kevin sent her an email instead of bothering me. Then she forwarded the email.

"What in the actual…" My jaw dropped. This had to be a fucking joke. A sick, goddamned joke.

Twenty-Two

I LIKED IT; OF course, I did, but the location was so suspect, it made me shiver. ME. SHIVER. I felt like I was officially on a real stalker's list. Obviously, that wasn't the case. Kevin was just doing his job, just like we' asked. It just so happened I loved the building this office was in. The problem was the proximity to the McLaughlin sisters' apartment.

The brick building with two floors and a small parking lot sat just across the street from them. This would be Julie's office, no doubt, if she agreed to it.

"Jules," I called to the reception area.

"I do, yes," came the knowing response.

"When we close today?"

"Yes, please."

Easiest decision ever? I'd have voted yeah. I didn't remember if I ever told Julie that's originally where I wanted the office to be, but if we liked the space, it would be hers. I'd grown fond of this office, and to be truthful, I'd bitch even more about the traffic situation at the new location. And at least until I killed Jimin and Suk, I couldn't be stationed there. Too close in proximity. Not okay.

When the day ended, I offered to drive up and bring Julie back to her car, but she said she had a meeting to go to, so we drove separate. Kevin met us there. He had to; he knew the access code for the lockbox. I'd been in a few of the offices in here, so I knew what the majority looked like. This one was no different than those.

Julie loved it, as suspected. We gave Kevin the go-ahead, and that was that. Julie ran off to her meeting, afraid to be late. I guessed it was one with the social worker. Otherwise, I didn't think she'd be so excited. I couldn't even pick out anything for a child because I wasn't sure if I'd be spoiling a teenager or a younger child. I'd already promised myself I'd help her and Cody in any way I could, and I meant it.

Kevin left, too, mumbling something about a date night as we hugged. He said he'd let me know when we could movie in, but to start getting a list of furniture together—we'd likely be moving in by the end of the month.

That gave me two weeks. It was quite perfect. After we moved in, tax season would be over, and I'd be able to do my thing. I hated waiting. But it seemed a new trend with me that I chose those I had to wait for in some way or another. *Note to self—no more accountants unless it's after tax season.*

For now, I'd study my prey and the kill-and-dispose location. Time would move slow, and I'd have to deal with that. Not such a big issue anymore. At least not now that I had techniques to use to reign in my escaped patience. Still, I'd follow the girls on the weekends. These were my thoughts as I grumbled aloud about the shit traffic I was now stuck in.

When it started moving again, I used my turn signal to switch lanes. Somehow, here in the universe of Florida, that was unacceptable to the car I had a pickup's amount of space to get in front of with my four-door Jeep. They honked and gave me the finger. I laughed at their lack of depth perception and hit the gas. I gained speed as this asshat gained on me. Okay, if they want to play games, let them. I'd be cool with a road rage case. Shit, I'd just been stalked again, so why not keep the crazies coming.

Then it happened. My first encounter with some jackass to get out of their vehicle.

We were stopped at a red light in Carrollwood when the guy I'd used my turn signal to get in front of came running up to my door. It was locked and the window was up, but I heard his creative use of profanities. When he stopped yelling and started panting, I rolled the window down and told him I carry. I was even sweet and polite about it. He shut up and took off to his car as best he could. I laughed it off, largely because he was mad I used my blinker. People were strange, Floridians even stranger.

I walked through my door well after six to a near-deafening screech from Minion. She didn't stop until I fed her, and even as she chomped away, she still made disgruntled noises at me.

"Sorry, kid. Had shit to do." I petted her, and she grumbled some more. Then I opened the fridge to find dinner for me. Leftover Thai sounded like luxury right now. And if I didn't eat it before tomorrow, I'd have to trash it. I hated trashing good food, so I ate it. It was better fresh, but still delicious reheated.

I wanted to get to the office early tomorrow to finish up today's paperwork and maybe avoid a line like today. My head hit the pillow early.

I was at the office by seven-thirty, which would give me enough time to finish the data entry for Barb and Julius and emailing of paperwork for Julius. I clacked away at the keyboard for about an hour before I was able to send the finalized paperwork to the lawyer. I was kind of OCD about triple-checking what I entered into my system and the payroll system. I was human and misspelled just like everyone else, but I wanted to keep mistakes to a minimum. I had a sterling image and reputation to uphold.

No sooner had I hit Send on the email than Julie came in, causing me to look at the clock in the lower right corner of my screen. Relief flooded me. It was quarter 'til nine. I was ready for the day, and glad Julie was always here on time.

We had time to go over our first appointment, who was scheduled for nine. This one would be Julies' interview, as would the rest. I'd chosen my assistant and would choose a backup from the list once interviewed. We liked to choose our own interviewees, and now that I had Barb under contract for a trail, I didn't expect to need another assistant, but I liked to be prepared.

The day moved along, interview after interview. Neither Julie nor I was thrilled or impressed by anyone enough to want to call them back for a second interview. Julie called and scheduled the three or four people we did want second interviews with. We had openings for them Thursday and Friday. Julie also pulled the remaining ads, confident we'd both have our new assistants training by the start of next week.

It was a little strange that we were so comfortable hiring someone and opening an office at the same time. To have staff who weren't fully trained was bad, but I also knew Barb would pick right up on the position and we could always push back the opening date of the new office. We still had furniture to pick out, and I had computers to order. I was glad I opened a corporate account with HP. Even with my smaller orders, I still got a better discount than I would have if I'd gone through one of the big-box stores.

I made the call, ordering one desktop like mine, one like Julie's, and two like the basic models out in the reception area. I essentially asked them to replicate my last order. All the same software, setup, everything. It all needed to be identical. I was given the price and informed I'd be billed.

"Okay. Thanks. You're wonderful," I said as I hung up. The transaction usually went well, and I used the same sales rep, who was always a down-to-business but delightful person to work with.

I knew I'd need to call the IT guy, too, just to have him make sure everything I asked for was set up properly. If not, HP usually credited me. Like most companies, they want their customers to be happy with their product.

I walked out into the reception area and pulled up a chair next to Julie.

"So, how did last night go?"

"Ugh," she sighed, "the kids were either terrified of us or hated us. We couldn't even have a simple conversation with any of them. One girl looked at me like she was going to slap me. This is so hard. I don't know if I can take the rejection much longer."

"Jules"—I put my hand on hers—"take a minute to think about how they feel. They feel rejected, too, I'd guess. They're in the foster system, and I'm sure they've met so many people who would prefer little kids under, like, eight that they're jaded. Maybe see if Maria could give you more background info on the next group you go meet so you're better prepared? I'm sure she can only tell you so much because of red tape and legalities, but it doesn't hurt to ask her."

Julie gave me a quick, meaningful hug. "You're probably right. I didn't even consider what these kids are going through, let alone what happened for them to be in foster care. Thinking about that makes me want to adopt them all, or at least do more to help them in general. Maybe I'll look into something—"

I cut her off with a raised hand. "You're getting a tad ahead of yourself. One step at a time. If I only brought back one lesson from China, that's it. I've never been the person to take things one at a time, but it helps ease the stress and impatience. Just breathe. Everything will work out. You'll see."

Julie looked downright embarrassed then cleared her throat and took a deep breath.

"I feel so much better now. I forget that you feel scattered a lot, too, and I always wondered how you handled it."

"Well, compartmentalization and therapy, honestly. I don't see Ben anymore, but I do call him from time to time. He helped me figure out if I really wanted and needed another office. I'm sure he'd see you—if you wanted."

Speaking of that compartmentalization, I seemed to have screwed that up with my feelings for Stu. Though they felt like they were now safely locked away. The true test would be to hang out with him in a one-on-one setting, like my house or his. I didn't want to push anything, but I made a mental note to try to see him before I finished the sisters off. Which would be here sooner than I realized.

Julie and I called it a day just before we actually closed the office—a whopping five minutes before. But in Tampa traffic, five minutes determined if you'd get home at a reasonable time or if you'd be stuck in the suck. On my drive home, I called Stu on the Bluetooth.

"Hey, Brit!" He sounded excited to hear from me. Now I was nervous.

Twenty-Three

THIS CAN'T BE GOOD. I'm now losing grip on the compartmentalization I was just patting myself on the back for. Breathe, girl, breathe.

"Hey Stu." I prayed to whatever could hear it that he didn't hear the quiver in my voice. "When do you want to have lunch or coffee or whatever? I was thinking we could maybe grill at my house or something."

"That sounds great! I'll check my work schedule and let you know later. How are you? Feeling better, I hope."

"So much, thanks to you. We've been crazy busy at the office. Would you believe a bunch of people showed up just to meet 'The Crazy Flame'? Man, I was pissed. Honestly, I'm still annoyed with the media for that. Then again, at least they didn't waste a good song on me."

Stu laughed.

I felt the weight lift. Maybe I would feel that much better when we hung out.

"How are you? We haven't really talked since, well…"

"I'm better than I thought I'd be. Been keeping busy, so that's probably helping, too."

"Same. It's all been intentional, except those people and the media circus. I may need to steal you from the force and hire you as my bodyguard if this shit keeps up."

We shared an awkward laugh.

"Okay, I went too far. Sorry. I thought it was funny."

"Oh, it is, but you really do need to start taking your personal safety seriously. I saw a video of some guy threatening a driver at an intersection. I recognized the Jeep being yelled at," he admonished me, concern clear in his tone.

"Fuuuuuuck. Really? Someone posted that?" Not good. Not good at all. I suddenly wanted to set the entire county ablaze just to keep people from my business.

"Don't worry, I'm a cop. It's been taken down."

"Thanks for handling that for me. I now feel like I can't even live my life without cameras."

"Well, you'll be happy to know your face wasn't in the video *and* no one recognized your Jeep. At least, no one who doesn't know you. Some people you know asked for the video to be removed as well, but the socials weren't having it until the cops stepped in. It's ridiculous. But you're safe; that's all that matters."

"Stu, I really don't know what to say. You've saved me twice now, like I'm some living damsel-in-distress cliché."

He chuckled.

"Okay, Stu. Let me know what works for you, and we'll plan it. I'm just getting home. Be safe!"

"You too, Brit."

He ended the call so I didn't have to. I felt better, but talking to him sucked a bit. Much less than the last time we talked, but it still sucked. It could've felt worse. I was grateful it didn't. I still, however, felt like a massive jerk. The feeling would pass, just like all the others did. At least Passing Through was about to open a second office.

Thinking about that made me proud and sad all at once. I'd be losing Julie, but that was really just me and my selfishness. I wanted her in my office, not another one. I also knew she'd rock the hell out of that office and make me even prouder of her than I already was. The internal conflict was overbearing. I needed a jog.

I ran inside, fed Minion, changed, and grabbed my Bluetooth earbuds in record time. I took off with a burst I wasn't aware I had to expend. I jogged until the sun went down, which wasn't smart. Bayshore was problematic enough by itself. The dark magnified the danger. I could've been on fire, and someone would have still hit me. That's what happens on a winding road where drivers don't pay attention or can't see. The city and county were trying to make safety improvements for pedestrians, but it wasn't enough. The only thing that *might* save pedestrians at night would be to close the road down. But that was impossible; Bayshore led directly into MacDill Air Force Base. Spike strips were my choice, but when I suggested it to the mayor, she thought I was kidding. I let her have that.

I showered under the hottest water the water heater allowed. Nope. Still felt the turmoil and hated every second of it. I remembered Ben telling me once to embrace the negative feelings instead of fighting them. Acknowledge them and let them fly away.

I tried; I really did. Then the frustration got to me, and I broke down, sobbing, on the tiled shower floor. I didn't know what was worse, being cold or having feelings. There never seemed to be an in-between for me. One extreme or the other. I liked the cold extreme. It allowed for so much more productivity than the warm. The warm rarely brought more than frustration. Sure, I had friends; the warm helped me earn them. But every killer needed to outwardly look like they blended in.

I didn't stand back up until the water ran cold. I resolved to run just as cold—to be my old self. I wouldn't change to my friends or those who knew me well, but I would stuff things back into their mental boxes and not let them fuck me over like this again. I was a fighter, and if it was my heart I need to fight, so be it.

Shivering as I toweled off, Minion came running in, screaming at me, rubbing up against my damp legs. She must have felt my mood and came to rescue me. Cats were mostly good about things like that. It was part of why I chose cats over dogs. This cat, though…Damn, she got needy. Tonight, it seemed I was the needy one. I needed to break down and cry; I needed to make the decision I made; I needed to get back to work.

I changed and went to Northdale, which was useless for another two or so weeks, but I needed to feel like I was doing the right thing. And I was. The girls were outside on the patio again when I parked. The night was a nice one—rare, given the time of year—and I should've been outside enjoying it, too. I did. My jog earlier and now with a nice breeze through my open windows.

Suk had changed the shade of her highlights to a bolder, brighter red. Jimin's hair was the same. It was as though Suk wanted to feel younger again. I could see that; I was around midlife crises frequently, given my clientele. I also noted, when I first happened upon them, that Suk looked older than she likely was. I was right, and if she wasn't such a twat, I might have felt bad. Hah. No more of that.

I watched until they turned the lights out, giving the appearance they went to bed. At least that was what I presumed. I sat there for another hour or so, taking in the silence and lack of people around.

Taking them from here would be too simple. I almost relished this knowledge. But I knew better than to get cocky. That's when things went wrong in a hurry. And that went for every aspect of my life. I drove slowly, taking that long way through the complex to get out. Not one person was out. Just how I liked it.

Twenty-Four

WEDNESDAY, OR HUMP DAY, as some people chose to call it. I wasn't much of a fan of that nickname, but it didn't matter what I thought. What mattered was that I had too much time before my KKD could become reality. I needed to catch them separately, to avoid one attempting to call for help while I knocked out the other. They partied on the weekends, so I could take them drunk, magnifying the ketamine effect. I liked that idea.

I'd already picked out the bushes I'd hide behind while I waited for their ride to leave. I had all I needed except the nylon rope. I wanted something to burn after getting blood on it, and peroxide eats away at nylon, but that's really all I could get my hands on. And it burned anyway. I had the trusty barrels down in Ybor, but I wasn't killing or disposing of the girls in Tampa. I'd need another trip to Gainesville to find—no, I wouldn't. I'd noticed some steel trash barrels on campus. I could easily use one of them. I was sure there was a boiler room in at least one of the buildings; some were pretty old, so they had to. If not, there were plenty of other places to burn the only piece of evidence that might have blood on it.

The key card would also have to be burned. I didn't trust shredders. Which gave me another idea. The county holds a shredding day, so I could always drop it there with some blank paper to be shredded.

The plan was coming together nicely. Now to wait to put it in motion.

They *had* to be accountants. Of course, they did. Thanks, universe, for teaching me again that I need to figure out this patience bullshit. Ugh.

Kevin called to let us know he had the keys for the second office and I needed to sign the paperwork. I asked him to bring it this afternoon. He agreed.

We had a few more interviews for assistants today, and that would end our list of first interviews and a couple of seconds. Regardless, we'd slow down with people in and out by the time Kevin would arrive.

Julie prepped us for the last time, and the flood gates opened. For three hours, we questioned new and requestioned old. We hadn't planned to ask any of the new interviews back another day for seconds. Our intention was to ask them to come back that day or hold them over. We lucked out, though. We didn't like any of them enough to spend more time with them.

Once we finished the squad of second interviews, we narrowed it down to two, telling everyone we'd let them know by the end of the day. They all left satisfied and confident the position was theirs. This person would be Julie's Julie, so the final decision rested on her. She hated that but knew and understood the necessity. She'd get used to hiring and firing people. And if she didn't, she could always come back here.

By the time Kevin showed up with the lease, we'd eaten lunch, and Julie felt much more confident about picking someone. She ended up choosing Shelly if Barbra decided to stay here with me. I already wanted Barbra anyway, and

Julie knew that. I knew that Julie could train anyone to be her assistant because I'm the picky one. I'm also the owner, and there are days I'm not here and need someone I can trust to run Passing Through.

We planned to train both women at the same time to make all of our lives easier. It would also make our choosing whom we wanted for ourselves simpler. Just because I liked Barbra for me didn't mean I wouldn't prefer Shelly. Those kinds of decisions were best made based on how well we got along and their work ethic, among many other things.

By the time Kevin left, Julie felt a lot better, though she was still nervous. That was understandable. I'd been where she was. Funny thing was I was nervous too. Would these new hires work out, or would we need to replace either or both in a week? Only way to tell was to let them work.

Julie already had "desks" bookmarked in her browser. I told her to place the orders she needed to. If she wanted to be in there ASAP, she needed everything—from desks to pens—ready.

As the days drew closer, Stu called me close to last minute. He wanted to have that lunch I'd asked about. He wanted to do it that weekend. It was perfect timing. I needed the mental break from waiting to knock off two very ignorant sisters and opening the new office. Stu and I also needed to know how we'd react if we hung out, just us. This was altogether a good plan.

Saturday arrived like a spaceship—out of nowhere and unexpected. Julie had hired her chosen, and a lot of money was put on the company credit card.

Now would be the true test of platonic, heterosexual relationships. Stu was on his way, and I was preparing the grill and chicken. I'd handle the rest later. I was drinking a glass of moscato when Stu came in. We may have been trying to tamp down our feelings for each other, but I wasn't going to let that stop our norms from being norms.

He came back into the kitchen and hugged me. He didn't bother to put down the bag he was carrying—the one that felt a lot like more wine and dessert. I hugged him back and took the bag before anything bad could happen to it. The quickness of the hug was also me resetting our boundaries. Stu seemed to understand that.

"What's been going on?" he asked, pulling the wine and dessert from the bag, careful to hide the dessert from me.

"Moving Julie into the new office. It sucks to be losing her, even though I'm not actually losing her. And dealing with the aftermath of this 'The Crazy Flame' bullshit. And what the shit is that nickname, anyway? A two-year-old could have done a better job."

We laughed. I tried to maneuver around Stu to see what he'd brought for dessert, but that didn't seem to work out. He was more agile than me and shoved it into the fridge before I could get a peek.

"What's been going on with you?"

"Same shit. Work hasn't been too busy, but it hasn't been as much fun as when you get stalked," he laughed.

I rolled my eyes.

"But mostly, I've been trying to reign in how I feel about you. I respect our friendship too much to ever force anything onto you, even protection."

"Well, thanks, I think. Stu, you know I'm big on personal safety, so the jabs can keep coming there," I giggled and handed him the plate of chicken. "Now, please get to work."

He smiled and did just that while I pulled out the sides and made a salad.

It was a great afternoon shared with an amazing friend. I truly adored him, and it was shitty I had motive to keep him around that had nothing to do with being friends or lovers. When he finally left, he kissed me on the cheek and thanked me for a great time. We promised to do it again soon, and the voice in my head said it would be after I dispatched the sisters.

Twenty-Five

There were no hitches or setbacks for Julie opening the new office, save one: She had so many applicants, she didn't know what to do with them. We didn't have enough openings for all of them. It didn't help that they didn't drive. Public transportation in the upper part of the county was atrocious, and that was being nice. She felt bad, but we kept their information on file for up to six months, company policy. It was up to them to keep us informed of their availability.

It was also a time for me to celebrate. The end of tax season. Or the end of the sisters. They'd be missed by their party friends, but those people were always so fucked up on alcohol and drugs, I doubted they'd realize Jimin and Suk were even missing.

When I'd bumped into the sisters in the bathroom that night, I noticed they had rings of white powder around their nostrils. Heroin or cocaine; it didn't matter. The amount of alcohol the two consumed rendered the twenty-minute highs useless anyway—at least it had in my experience. What a waste. Of what could be two decent human beings. Shame they were so sickeningly cruel toward their adopted country and ignorant to anything artistic. Philistines, both of them. They may have come off all "hookers and blow and 'Murica," but that would be an outright lie.

They were the hunted and I, the hunter. As dull as it was to watch them, I'd do it. I'd plan the perfect night to end their lives and get my precious high. I gave up long ago trying to figure out what caused the endorphin rush. Hell, there was likely more than endorphins involved anyway. I wasn't a neuroscientist and didn't want to be. I just knew that there were hormones and chemicals involved in different states of euphoria—I was a teenager once, just like everyone else, and had a drug education class in high school.

The first Friday the new office was open, Julie and I met our friends out at The Pub. It'd been too long since we had a proper girls' night. We also had a reason to celebrate. And man, did we.

It started off with all of us catching up, the girls relaying their concerns about me and congratulations to Julie and me. I thanked Julie for the growth of Passing Through; if it hadn't been for her being so amazing and trustworthy and every other good thing I valued in an assistant, there wouldn't be a second office.

My toast made her tear up. We clinked, and Julie made her announcement, to the rest of the girls, about being approved to adopt a child. I bounced in my seat like a child, I was so excited she decided to share the news. More clinking.

In turn, each woman at the table shared updates and victories and losses. Overall, everyone experienced more victories. We finally gave up the clinking and cheered instead, followed by sips or chugs. Julie, and I had been so stressed trying to hire assistants and get the office open, we chugged.

We enjoyed a long overdue night of good food, good friends, and good drinks. We stayed until they kicked us out, tipping generously for our usual top-notch service. I asked them to name the room after us, or at least the table, since we were there so much. The manager laughed. I did, too, though

I wasn't sure if I was joking or not. We made a deal that when I was sober, we'd talk about it. We ladies hugged each other goodbye and thanked each other for such a great night.

Devin was working valet that night, so I asked him to take Julie and me back to my house. When we got there, Julie shuffled to the guest room, stopping to feed Minion on her way. I heard her flop on the bed with a sound of exasperation mixed with total happiness. Then, she started snoring.

Giggling, Devin and I went to my room and got down to our delinquent playtime. There was no talking, other than things one would usually say during times like these. We went for hours. When we were finished, exhaustion took hold, and we started to drift off, Devin's head on my chest. We were as sweaty as though we'd just finished working out. I mean, we did just work out. We burned *a lot* of calories. We were too worn out and content to be bothered with anything other than closing our eyes.

I heard a voice, muffled at first, gaining clarity the more I woke. I first thought it was a dream, but that wasn't the case. There was someone talking. And then someone else. There was a conversation going on in my house, and I'm in my bed half-asleep. What the hell? Then I remembered last night and opened my eyes. No Devin. His was one of the two voices. The other was Julie. They were heatedly discussing something. I couldn't quite hear.

I followed my habits and went downstairs after. There was a fresh pot of coffee, Devin was cooking something on the stove, and Julie sat at the table miffed and telling Devin something about "That's not how you make it."

"Morning," I giggled and grabbed a cup of coffee. "Jules, what's got you in a twist?"

"He's making the eggs wrong," she huffed.

I snorted laughing. "Really? That's what you're mad about?"

"Well, yeah. They're gonna turn out like shit."

"WHOA!" Devin and I said in unison.

"I think that's the first time I've ever heard you cuss, Jules," I said, my mouth still hanging open a bit. Devin looked at me, shrugged his shoulders, and threw more butter in the eggs like Julie commanded.

"Sorry. I'm a little hungover. Besides, the butter makes the eggs more…eggy," she sputtered.

"Like my eggs?"

'YES! Just like yours! Brit, teach him how to make your eggs? Please?"

"Damn, okay, if you want them that bad, you got it. Will you pull the bacon out?"

"Yep!" Julie jumped up from her chair so fast, I thought either she or the chair were falling over, but she held her ground. So did the chair.

Shaking my head, I hip-bumped Devin aside and took over cooking duties. Within thirty minutes, we had half a pound of bacon cooked, eggs ready, and hot coffee. Julie licked her lips and dug in. Devin tended the remaining bacon in the oven, and I ate as well. I loved mornings like this. But I couldn't allow myself the joy on a constant basis. I knew I was easily annoyed, and I wasn't risking getting caught over something as simple as a breakfast gathering.

It truly was sad, from an outsider's perspective. From mine, however, it was perfection.

Twenty-Six

DEVIN TOOK JULIE AND me back to International to pick up our vehicles. We all parted ways from there, me bent on showering. Julie had an appointment to go meet some kids and Devin had homework.

The McLaughlin sisters weren't part of anything last night at The Pub, which meant they'd either be there or elsewhere tonight. I wasn't sure I cared enough to follow, but I decided I would anyway. They could have fun spots I'd yet to go to. I spent the day running to Lowe's for rope and packing my bag. I was more than ready but not entirely prepared. I still needed to know their habits aside from the work week.

The drive to Northdale from today until I took the sisters would feel like forever. The drive to Gainesville would feel like a twelve-hour ride when in all reality it was around two hours. I was excessively hungry for this. I'll admit I was nervous, too. This would be my first dual kill, and I had such grand plans. They would watch each other suffer like the swine they were. That was a horrible reference; pigs really do get a bad rap, and I liked pigs. They helped me out with Brody, and they were quite friendly. They were pretty damn clean, too—cleaner than most people, I'd venture.

I sat for hours, waiting, watching. I ate half an egg salad sandwich and a handful of cashews. The girls weren't home.

Odd. It was a Saturday afternoon. Whatever. I got out of my Jeep and walked around their building. I figured tonight could be the night. If not, I could wait another week, but the KKD *had* to take place on a Saturday. I just had a gut feeling that Saturday would be the best day. Add to that the fact the girls partied on Saturday nights, and, well, it wasn't fucking rocket science.

I knew their ride wouldn't be gone until they hit the top of the stairs at their door. Lucky for me, there was also a storage closet at the top of those stairs. Even better for me that one of the girls had a thing for potted plants. That's where I would hide. Behind the plant in the corner between the half wall and closet. Even lit by the outside lamp on the wall, that corner was dark enough not to be seen through.

Neighbors had potted plants placed in the same spots. I supposed it was the easiest way to make sure they got proper sunlight and rain but were out of the way of the front door. I didn't care; they weren't my plants. But they held the key to being unseen.

As the sun set, I sat for a little while by one of the man-made lakes near their building. I contemplated how far I'd come and how far I still had to go. With everything from being the best serial killer I could be to being the best me I could be. Even being the coldest tolerable version of myself came into by thoughts. I really did want Stu in my life more, but I couldn't allow that to come to fruition. *What was my deal with cops?!*

The sun was fully behind the horizon when I got back to my Jeep, glancing up at the apartment that housed my quarry. The lights seemed to be on a timer, something I'd noticed before but thought the girls were just OCD about turning lights on at a specific time. I was also preoccupied by my feelings the last time I was here. Feelings that had been assaulted and forced back into their box. My life wasn't a game, but if I needed to treat my hobby like it was, I damn well would.

I'd only just gotten comfy and settled in for what I anticipated to be a few hellish hours when an SUV pulled up and Suk fell out followed by Jimin. Jimin was stumbling. FUCK! I missed my chance to lie in wait! Maybe I could salvage this. The SUV pulled away quicker than the others the girls had come home in, making me think the driver wanted nothing else to do with them. I got out of my Jeep and snuck across the lot as they tripped up the stairs. I was there behind them by the time they'd successfully balanced themselves on the fourth from the bottom.

I stuck Jimin first since she was more sober, then Suk. They both dropped in seconds, tumbling to the cement pad at the landing of the stairs. I stood over them, giggling. They were a heap of flesh, clothes, and general dishevelment. I couldn't tell who was on whom, and it didn't really matter. I grabbed the one on top, who turned out to be Jimin, duct-taped her mouth, then tied her hands together. I duct-taped her ankles together to cause more pain when it came off, more than any other reason.

Suk was next, and I bound her the exact same way. These two would be out for hours, so I ran for my Jeep, backing it into a spot close enough to their stairs. Then I hauled each one up and around my neck like a human scarf and over to the cargo area of my Jeep. It was already lined with plastic from…I don't remember when I did that, but it was great that it was done. I hoped that wasn't left over from Brody. Not that it would be the worst thing, but dangerous, nonetheless. Again, I risked fucking up bad enough to get caught. Dammit!

Once they were piled in, I closed the door and jumped behind the wheel. I made a left out of the complex and onto North Dale Mabry Highway toward State Road 54. I made a right at that intersection, driving east to I-75. Then came the left onto I-75. What took a mere thirty minutes felt like an hour. I settled down as much as I could and drove the speed limit. Troopers were known to hang out for those going anything over the posted seventy. Some were more lenient than others, allowing for five over, but I had just kidnapped my first duo and had no intentions of being caught.

Two hours later, I backed into a spot near the meat processing facility. I hopped out of my Jeep and did a quick walk-around to make sure no one else was around. My SO-COM friend said he'd be monitoring the cameras for my arrival. I could only hope he put them on a loop of nothing and no one—like the way it was now—by the time I used the key card to enter. When I did, the door opened to a clean white hallway lined with windows and doors. I walked in, the automatic door closing behind me, and crept down the hall, looking for the right room.

Twenty-Seven

FINDING THE ROOM, I readied it for what I had planned. I found two hooks with nothing on them and slid them so they faced each other. Then I went back out to my Jeep and unloaded whichever sister was on top and brought her into the room, hanging her on a hook by her tied-up wrists. I did the same to the other sister.

Slapping Jimin then Suk awake, I saw their eyes light up with terror at being tied up and duct-taped, pleading to each other for help. I laughed and stepped between them. In unison, they looked from me back to each other. Suk showed a flash of recognition in her eyes. I pulled the tape from her mouth, and she screamed from the pain.

"You," she spat. "You were in the bathroom that night at The Pub!"

"Correct. That's why you're here now." My eyes and tone were icy. "You two will suffer for your ignorance. I've been watching you and your dull lives. You're here to make money and party, something you couldn't do where you came from. That's not why your parents brought you here, and disrespecting them like this—being disgustingly ignorant to the culture you live in, the one they brought you to for a better life—deserves to be punished. Lucky for you, I've got that covered."

I leaned over to Jimin and took the tape from her mouth. She screamed. I laughed again. Then I squatted down, slowly removing the tape from one ankle.

"What are you doing to her," Suk cried indignantly.

"The same thing I'll be doing to you in a minute," I replied, putting gloves on.

I pulled a knife from the back of my waistband and flicked it open. It had a freshly sharpened edge but didn't reflect. It was one with a black oxide coating, purposely designed to not reflect. More for cops and military, but civilians were able to buy it, too.

I grabbed the bare ankle of Jimin and held it for just a moment. Long enough to let true fear sink in while a puddle of yellow formed around her other foot. Then I pulled the knife across the back of her ankle. She screeched so loud, I thought she might shatter the glass. Suk screamed out for her sister. I stood and looked at her, smiling.

I then squatted back down and removed the tape from the opposite ankle, slicing it open just like I did to Jimin. Suk screeched.

Both of the girls squirmed and wriggled, trying to break free, but with one Achilles and posterior tibial artery severed each, there was no way they would make it out of here alive. I wouldn't allow that.

Suk looked down at me, at the pool of blood forming below her. She screamed again, fighting harder against the rope that bound her wrists. The pool grew the more she fought. The more she fought, the more lifeless she became. Jimin looked on with horror and stopped struggling.

Suk was near passing out when I sliced her other ankle open. She bled slower than when I first cut her. Jimin cried out something not in English.

"Are you calling me names? Cursing me out? Not that it matters. You'll bleed out just like your sister is doing."

I stood and walked over to her. She kicked out, weakened by the loss of blood, and connected with my shin. I grabbed her ankle, stepped back far enough for my clothes to not be bled on, and sliced her other ankle. I removed the remaining duct tape from both girls and placed it in a contractor bag. One that would be burned somewhere around here.

I didn't have to wait long before the girls' hearts no longer spat blood from their ankles. I hoisted Suk off her hook first and placed her on a clean, stainless-steel cutting table and went to work with the tools that were available. It took me around two hours to cut her up small enough to fit the pieces into the meat grinder. Her clothes were still on when I began cutting her up but fell off in pieces that I picked up and placed in the burn bag.

Once Suk was sausage, I packaged her up to sell, mimicking the already packed-to-sell sausages. I even printed a label and stuck it on the package. Jimin was next on the cutting table, followed by grinding, and packaging. In all, it took me over six hours to kill and dispose. I wandered the building, looking for an incinerator. I found the room, which struck me as odd, since I hadn't found a smokestack coming from this building. Maybe I didn't look hard enough. I'd have my shit back together by the next kill. I had to.

I threw the bag in along with my gloves, pulled on a fresh pair, and pushed the button. Soon there was nothing left, not even melted plastic. That was a hot fire; I wanted one of my own.

I still needed the key card to exit, so I figured I'd dispose of that in some other fashion. For now, I needed to get the hell out of here and on the road back home. I jumped in my Jeep and drove as expected off the campus. I didn't speed now for the same reasons I didn't speed earlier—detection. *Just be normal, and all will be fine*, I thought.

Traffic on the drive home wasn't so bad. I expected it to be heavier than it was. Lucky for me, I supposed. At least the two-hour drive didn't feel like it took longer. I enjoyed my euphoria the rest of the day. So much so that I even had a hard time calming down once I got home. Minion screamed at me, her usual reaction to leaving her for hours, and I picked her up to calm her down. She wasn't thrilled when I set her on the bed so I could change and put my bag back in the safe in my closet. I even put the key card in there until I was calm enough to evade suspicion when going to Ybor to destroy it.

I sent Devin a message asking what he was doing and grabbed a glass for some wine. Devin responded, and we had a brief conversation. Twenty minutes later, my glass empty, me still euphoric, the doorbell rang. I'd never had post-kill sex before, and I wanted to try it.

Amazing was an understatement. I couldn't find the right descriptors for the sensations or the mind-blowing finale. This was something I could get used to. I just needed a boy toy who didn't sniff around and knew his place. If Devin could kill his feelings for me, I think he could stick around for a while.

Twenty-Eight

THERE WAS NO NEWS other than a pair of sisters went missing. Because of their age, there was nothing on the news about them for over a week. In that week, I'd been mildly amused by the lack of information. Even Stu had nothing about missing twenty-something professionals. I guessed their friends really didn't miss them after all. It was the apartment complex who reported them missing when they attempted to contact them for overdue rent.

Stu suspected nothing. No one did. I was more than happy with that.

Julie came into the office one day for lunch. We sat in the kitchen eating and chatting when she broke down. Tears streamed down her face when she looked up at me.

"Jules, what's wrong?"

"My cat died. He was fine one day, and the next…I found him when I got home from work. Applesauce was lying on the couch with him." She sniffed and wiped her face.

"Oh no! I'm so sorry." I went to hug her, and she gratefully accepted. We stayed that way for a while. Tears rolled down my face, too; I never met the cat, but I knew he was Julie's baby. Seeing her in pain made the heart I worked so hard to hide hurt. It was the circle of life.

Julie sniffled again and perked up. "But I do have some good news. We met a child we adore, and he adores us. The paperwork has been started."

"What! That's better than good news! That's fabulous! How old is he? What's his name? Come on, I need details. I need to spoil my new nephew."

Julie started telling me about Brian, the boy she and Cody were trying to adopt, and she almost turned into a cartoon she was so animated. Brian was twelve, almost thirteen. His parents couldn't afford to keep him, so they gave him up in the hope of him finding a loving home. I listened, looking for possible signs of trouble that may have been hidden in the details. She gave me none.

I was so excited for Julie and Cody that I almost forgot the cat died. Julie seemed to also, until she stopped talking about Brian. She cried again, and I held her.

"I'll go to the vet with you, if you'd like."

"Thanks. Cody and I already had him cremated. His urn is in his favorite window."

I shed a few more tears with her. "What about a girls' night? My house? Before you bring Brian home. It'll be a celebration of life and a real celebration. Or we can make it a real party at Osten's house. What do you say?"

"I like the girls' night thing. We can have a real party when Brian is comfortable with it. I think that's fair." She stopped talking to think and looked like she was in space. Julie stayed like that for many minutes.

"Oh...wow. I have a son." The shock and awe in her voice gave way to pure pride. "I have a son, Brian. He's twelve."

Happy tears choked me up for the first time in my life. I'd never felt this way—not that I could recall, anyway. I'd brought one of the greatest, nicest, most deserving people into my office and my life. Julie was my friend and protégée.

Now here she sat, ridiculously happy and running the second office of Passing Through. I wasn't sure life could get any better. Even Barbra and Shelly were working out well for us.

With how great life had suddenly become, something in my gut still felt off. Not wrong, but off. Like it was all too good to be true. I wanted to revel in the joy with Julie, not be a downer, but my life experience hadn't been filled with much real joy, and my instincts about things going wrong were usually right. I set it aside. I knew what could happen, and I wasn't ignoring it. I just wanted to feel things I'd never felt until now.

Then my cell rang. It was my SOCOM friend. I hit the button to ignore it, and he called right back. I excused myself and answered it.

"Brit, I scrubbed the recordings, but you have to get rid of that key card."

"Say what now? How do you know I still have it?"

"You underestimate me. Send it back to me, and I'll handle it."

"So black ops," I joked, "sorry, this actually isn't even close to funny. Tell me the drop, and I've got it covered. Also, thanks again."

He told me how to wrap it up and where to "trash" it and hung up. Something told me if I tried to call back I'd get a recorded message saying the number was no longer in service. I love how he's so incredible with these things, and I wished I could be the same. I accepted I wasn't and couldn't and left it at that. If I needed his help again, I knew he'd be there.

I went back to Julie and apologized for the interruption.

"No worries." She glanced at her watch. "I should get back anyway. And we're still on for girls' night." She smirked then, hugged me.

Julie was barely out the door when I hit Send on the group text asking if Saturday would be a good night for everyone to come to my house.

Saturday arrived, and so did the girls. Danielle brought along a newbie, Shaelyn. Danielle was training Shaelyn—Shae, as she asked us to call her—to take over her spot in the company. Danielle was being promoted, again. Talk about all kinds of celebration going on. I successfully killed two, Julie had a son, Danielle was getting another promotion, and Stu, sweet Stu, was dating again. It hurt, but we couldn't be together. Not now, probably not ever. He promised to introduce us as soon as he knew her better.

Shae was a lot of fun. We all liked her. The night was rowdy and full of drunk women. It turned club-like in a hurry. We all danced and drank and sang. Overall, it was a great night. There were only two of us left awake by 2 a.m.—Julie and me. I didn't think she could hang like that.

"Jules, I didn't know you could drink like that."

"Hah," she laughed, "I sipped my drinks while the rest of you went to town. I can't drink like I used to, and I shouldn't anyway. I know it's girls' night and that's part of the plans for the night, but I don't really want to be hungover tomorrow. I want to enjoy the day with my family."

I smiled and hugged her hard. I was so glad life was good to her.

Shae heard us talking and came into the kitchen to join us. That girl came prepared. Literally. She brought an air mattress. I initially thought that an odd thing, but it was quite genius. If you ended up needing to crash somewhere, at least you *knew* you'll be comfortable. If I didn't drive dead and/or unconscious people around, I'd consider it. Or maybe I'd just trade my Jeep in for a different SUV. Hah! That was funny. I'd survive without one in the back of my Jeep.

Shae sat with us, almost falling into her chair, giggling.

"I'mmm still a little drunk," she giggled and hiccupped at the same time, which sounded painful.

"Why aren't you asleep? Is everything okay," I questioned. I wanted to make sure I'd done all I could to make sure she would still hang out with us.

"Oh yeah. Danielle snores pretty loud, and I'm a light sleeper. No bigs."

"Okay, cool. So, anything I can get you?"

"Nah, I'll grab another drink. Thanks. I think that drink will be water anyway." She hiccupped again, and her face turned red.

"Well, I think Julie and I are finally going to take a nap. If you need anything, feel free. Oh! And we usually have a group breakfast too. I hope you can stay for it. We'd all love to get to know you more." I hugged her, Julie waved, and we went up to sleep in my bed.

Once we were comfortable, Julie agreed about wanting to get to know Shae better and possibly including her in our girls' nights.

I hugged Julie and congratulated her again, then fell asleep.

Twenty-Nine

It turned out Shaelyn was a good singer. I didn't enjoy waking up to that, but hey, the girl was good. Strike one and note to self. Was it really a strike, though? Yes. Yes, it absolutely was. I imagine life with a morning person may be like this. I wouldn't know. I wasn't much of a socializer until I'd had a minimum of two cups of coffee.

Julie was even out of bed. I hoped she was downstairs making the eggs herself this time. No need to traumatize the new girl. I hesitated to get out of bed myself but did anyway. It wasn't like I couldn't nap later. In the meantime, I did invite Shae to stay for breakfast with us, so I would play the part of a good host.

By the time I got to the kitchen, though, all the girls were pitching in. Shae was singing made-up songs about coffee and the caffeine gods, Danielle was baking the bacon, Julie had control over the eggs, Kristen was setting the table, and Sarah and Heather had just walked in bearing two gallons of orange juice. *Well, looks like I'm not needed in my own house.* I could get used to that. I grabbed glasses for those who wanted juice or something else and set them on the table.

I laughed at Julie because any time Danielle went to open, or even looked at, the oven, she'd get super protective of the pot of eggs.

"Jules, they're scrambled eggs. Calm down," I managed between sips of coffee.

"I will NOT. You've done a fine job of spoiling me, Britney. Now the eggs must be perfect." She flourished the stirring spatula, flinging egg onto Danielle. Suddenly I had my own children to handle. Julie genuinely felt bad, while Danielle got defensive and accusatory.

As funny as this was to watch—knowing the girls would make up by the time they sat down to eat—I felt the need to jump in anyway, so I stood between the two. Julie kept swinging the spatula; that was really the only reason. Danielle was getting madder each time she wore more egg. We all called it egg abuse, and that ended Julie's agitation. We all burst into fits of laughter, some of us snorting, as Shae looked around at us, unsure if she was allowed to join in. I nodded when our eyes met, encouraging her to have fun. She joined, giggling, still awkward.

I made it a point during breakfast to hand her my phone so she could text herself from it. This ensured we'd have each other's numbers. I saved hers right away, and she waited until after we finished eating to save mine. I understood she didn't want to come off as rude. First impressions aren't always what they seemed.

Heather and Kristen had to get back home right after breakfast. Julie helped clear the table, then left to go home to Brian and Cody. Danielle wanted to stay but had to get some things in order before the workweek started, so I offered to take Shae home. Both agreed, and Shae hung out with me for a little bit longer.

We talked like we'd known each other a little longer than just meeting. Her favorite color was red, same as mine. She dropped out of college and worked her way up the cell phone company ranks on merit and ass-kissing. None of that surprised me. Neither did her confession about meat.

Shae said she'd always been intrigued by cannibalism and why it even started. I joked about Darwinism, but she corrected me. The girl was stone-faced about it. Not a hint of joking was acceptable. It was strange. When I went to look up if what she'd said was true, she started laughing.

"That was convincing." I eyed her like she was a cannibal.

"Sorry, I always do that to people," she said, while giggling, "to see how they react. Most people blanch and do whatever they can to get out of the conversation."

"I don't judge. We all have something we're into that others don't understand."

"What are you into, Brit?"

"Guns. I've got two so far. And a few knives. And I used to take Krav Maga lessons. I believe women should know how to defend themselves when necessary. Most people I know don't agree with it. More the guns and knives part than anything," I responded with a shrug.

"That's rude. Everyone's beliefs should be respected, even if they're different."

If she had half a clue.

"Well, I suppose I should get you back to your car. It's at Danielle's?"

"It is. Thanks, Brit, for letting me hang and not treating me like an outcast. It's so hard these days to make friends."

"I agree."

I grabbed my keys, and we left.

In my Jeep, Shae got lost in the scenery. It made me wonder how long she'd been in Tampa. Or if maybe she was lost in thought. We pulled up to Danielle's house about twenty minutes later, and she thanked me for the ride. She said she'd text me during the week and asked if we could hang out again.

"Of course! I'd enjoy getting to know each other. Let me know when you're free, and we'll set something up!"

I waited for her to pull away before I got out of my Jeep and knocked on Danielle's door. I wanted to know what her feelings were about Shae. Turns out, she was testing the girl. If someone could survive an overnight at my house with the group, they were pretty much good.

I felt something in my gut about Shae but couldn't put words to it. Nothing bad, just…off. She was sweet, but that could've been simply for show. I didn't bring any of this up to Danielle. I didn't want her to think bad of someone I'd only met twelve hours ago. My gut was usually right, but this was one of those cases where I didn't know what it was telling me other than "she's different."

Well, shit, I hoped she was different. I'm not friends with normal. None of my ladies were normies, and they loved it and me. We took pride in our ability to appear normal to those who we didn't want to know us very well or allow into our inner circle. We had other friends, but they weren't like us. That one movie said it well. "We *are* the weirdos." Yep, that's us. Minus the witchy parts.

Danielle went on to tell me how long she'd been searching for someone to take her position and that Shae was "damn-near perfect." Sounded right. Shae did tell me she was accustomed to brownnosing. I was sure she complimented Danielle and told her how she could improve upon things Danielle had built. And I was sure she would. Right after she tore them apart, piece by piece, to see how they worked and put them back together with her improvements inside. It's what I would do. Hell, I've done it to my own processes. It was called efficiency.

Satisfied with Danielle's assessment of Shae, I went home to nap and clean up.

Thirty

Shae texted me on Wednesday, apologizing for being late. I didn't think she was late, but I had no place to tell her that. Not yet. We decided to meet for lunch on Friday at some sushi place downtown. That's where the corporate office she and Danielle worked at was located. We set a time, and that was that. We didn't chat much between days. I knew Danielle's workdays were long sometimes and figured that was the case.

My suspicions were confirmed on Friday. Shae said they'd been working fourteen-hour days so she could learn as much as she dared. I admired her spirit.

"Don't you think that's burnout waiting to happen?"

"Maybe"—she took a piece of sushi roll in her chopsticks and dipped it in soy sauce—"but I've only got two weeks to absorb as much as I can direct from Danielle. Then she'll be near impossible to talk to if I need help."

I understood and respected that. It's what I'd do, too. And I'd likely shake off thoughts of burnout. But this work conversation was going nowhere, and I wanted to get to know the real Shae. So, I started asking questions. I went for the jugular from the gate.

"So, tell me about your ideal significant other," I smirked. "I don't date, and I like hearing what friends' standards are."

"Tall, dark, handsome, rich, old, black, white…I don't know that I have a type. But I can tell you this: I like men who are decent-enough-looking to want to be seen in public with, kind, forgiving—because I can be a real bitch, and I know it—and who have their own place and life somewhat together—"

I looked at her, waiting for her to finish. When she realized this, she said, "Oh, sorry. I can't think of anything else. It's all just basic things, though. Like, what I adore in one guy could annoy the shit out of me in another. It's weird…or maybe I am."

"If you're not weird, we can't be friends."

We mimicked toasting with our sushi rolls and ate happily. I mulled over what Shae said about a significant other. It sounded logical. I'd find her flaws one way or another and go from there. My gut still said something was off about her. I'd figure it out—today, tomorrow, a year from now. Time didn't matter right now; I didn't feel like I was having lunch with another killer. Shae was just a young woman trying to make her way in this world, strange or not.

We finished lunch and agreed to do it again soon. We parted ways, me still thinking over every detail that could've given me a clue about why I felt the way I did.

Nothing came to mind by the end of the workday, and Julie and I discussed having dinner, the four of us. I offered to cook, but she wasn't having it. Then I offered to have it at Joe's house, party or not. Still no, though she agreed to a party if I agreed to give her more time. Duh. She insisted she and Cody cook and I go there. I sighed when I caved, then forced her to let me bring dessert. It was like arguing with a family member over the last potato chip or something. I laughed and so did Julie. We set it up for this Friday night, two days away.

On Friday, we agreed to 7 p.m. because I wanted to go home and change and could an Uber or something. I was taking two bottles of wine, cheesecake, and some books. The books were for Brian. Julie said he enjoyed reading monster stuff, so I picked up a few books I'd heard a lot about. One was from an author writing an ongoing series that featured the same main character for over thirty years. The other was newer with a lot of geek and pop culture references I understood. I could geek out, too, though I didn't make that known.

I'd read a lot of the Dark Elf books and all of the others. To share those with others was a gift I gave every chance I could let my geek flag out. Monsters, dragons, warlocks, and other creatures existed in these books. It was fun to imagine if they existed in real life, too. Or maybe that was just me, hoping for a pet dragon to incinerate people with. I wasn't sure, and I didn't care. I just hoped Brian liked them.

He did. Squealing in excitement, he jumped up and down, thrilled to be given all these books. He'd wanted to read all of them, but his foster parents wouldn't allow it. Something about fantasy being the devil or evil. I couldn't wrap my brain around people like that, but he had been in their care at the time. I was happy he wasn't anymore because Aunt Brit the Closet Geek had come to the rescue. Even Julie was surprised I read the same books I'd given Brian.

"Look," I said, taking a bite of medium-rare steak and savoring the melty goodness, "I don't tell anyone about my secret reading habits. And I definitely do *not* want to hear about your romance obsession. As you know, I live my life without it."

The whole table laughed, even Brian. At twelve, the kid was really smart: book-smart and street-smart. It kind of worried me, him still being a kid and all, but it was probably due to the hard life he'd had up to that point.

He went on about how he begged his foster parents to let him learn self-defense and walk to school. It wasn't like they lived in a bad area, but Brian had friends who did, and his foster parents didn't approve. My parents didn't always approve of my friends either. I don't think anyone's ever did.

What mattered was that Brian was fairly well adjusted. He was happy too. Watching Julie, Cody, and Brian as a family warmed my cold heart. Okay, not much, but it made me see why I cared so damn much about Julie. I couldn't even begin to describe how amazing she was. The whole family, really. Cody worked hard and was super smart, landing some engineering job that he wanted even before he graduated. I was thankful to have them in my life.

After dinner, we drank coffee and talked. About anything we could. It felt like I was finally getting to know Cody, too, and how perfect a match he and Julie were.

Then I wanted to vomit. Seeing the ideal family made me as happy as it sickened me. That's what made me...me. It wasn't that I didn't appreciate these things. Quite the opposite. I appreciated and respected them, but it wasn't suitable for my lifestyle or wants to have one of my own.

Being a killer made me not want a lot of things my friends did or had. Romantic relationships and kids topped the list. Sure, I was more concerned about what would happen to me if I got caught. I imagine it would have negative effects on a boyfriend or kid, same as it would my father and Osten. I'd already let too many people into my life.

At least I had a reason to let Shae in.

Thirty-One

I LEFT JULIE AND Cody's house and went straight to my safe when I got home. I was annoyed by those warm, gooey feelings again and needed an outlet. If that outlet was finding a range that was open or maybe sorting through my bag to make sure I had enough supplies, I didn't care.

I did a quick internet search on my phone, not finding any open ranges at that hour. So I pulled my bag out and went through it and the supplies in the safe. I didn't note anything I needed, but I did feel better to run through the inventory. Somehow, sorting my supplies gave me more perspective. I preferred to be organized about it, anyway.

I was still itching to know more about Shae too. I went downstairs to find my laptop and see if she'd temped for me at any point. Nothing. I started to feel, on a deeper level, something wasn't right at all about her.

So what if she was weird or quirky or eccentric? Most, if not all, of my friends were. I refused to surround myself with rigid people. Flexibility meant more malleable, which was vital to making sure my omissions weren't picked up on. Being what I was, I was not of the school of omission equals lying. I did outright lie, and I did omit. It was rare I felt bad about doing either.

Back to thoughts of Shae. She was lying. I could feel it. A liar knows a liar. Did she know how good a liar I was? Chances were slim she even had a clue.

Actually, now that I thought about it, I wouldn't put it past her to pick up on the fact that I was a liar, but the extent was difficult to figure. Even for me and my own lies. I sometimes thought that would be my undoing. I'd lose track of things I said to the wrong person, and that would be the end of it for me. No appeals, no high-end lawyer like that one in Orlando. I'd take my death sentence with the knowledge that everyone I loved could be honest when they told people they never suspected a thing.

I would find out what Shae was hiding. One way or another. If she refused to tell me, I'd call in the cloak-and-dagger private investigators. I hoped it wouldn't come to that. If it did, oh well. I was that determined. Something about her wasn't right. It wasn't anything easy to pick up on, obviously. If it had been, I wouldn't have been racking my brain.

I closed the laptop and went to bed.

Saturday morning, I sent a text to all the girls to find out when they wanted to have another Pub night. I was hoping getting Shae to come out might do something to help ease my instincts. I was so wrong that I swore off hoping.

We went out the following weekend. Sat at our usual table upstairs and got Rachel, our usual server. The whole night was so usual that it wasn't. I felt like everyone except Julie was hiding something from me. I kept the wine flowing, but nobody spilled their secrets. It was a group secret; that much was plain. Then, I got Danielle to go to the bathroom with me, and she broke down.

"We wanted to throw Julie a party."

"I'm sorry, what? No. You all know that's MY job."

Danielle hung her head. "We do; that's why we were trying to keep it a surprise."

"Not cool."

I hugged her and reassured her I wasn't mad. I was pissed. No one needed to know.

When I got back to the table, I made it clear that if they tried that shit again, I probably *would* freak out. Julie was confused. The rest of the group wasn't. I tried to brush Julie's confusion off, but she wasn't having it.

"No, Britney. Tell me what you meant."

Sigh. "They were trying to overthrow me and plan a surprise party for you."

"Oh. OH! No!" She shook her head at everyone except me. "You don't understand. Brit's been trying to get a date out of me since we brought Brian home. No. This is her party to throw."

Everyone else nodded. Shae eyed me suspiciously.

Hah! You think I control them. Shows how perceptive you are not.

When the night ended and we'd all grabbed our vehicles from valet, Devin followed me home. I took my frustrations out on him, and he didn't complain. He seemed to enjoy it more than usual. Interesting. Mental note made.

I woke up the next day, and he was gone. There was a note on my nightstand apologizing for not being in my bed. It said something about a last-minute paper. I got that. I got that more than I'll admit. I only did that when it was necessary. Usually, because I just killed someone. I tried not to make it a habit.

Back in college, one professor was surprised by my late entry and emailed me to ask if everything was all right. The concern was unwanted, but I couldn't let him know, so I responded, thanking him and telling him I was overwhelmed with papers all due on the same day. I think I even said something about being unprepared.

Lies in college to professors about late-for-me papers weren't the ones that could build up. Not that it was all that long ago, but I'd been so careful to cover my tracks then and not be distracted. I also killed, maybe, twice in my whole college career. I was more concerned with graduating and being out in the world to really focus on being what I was. I kept it random and low on the radar.

I was bummed I couldn't take out more frustration on Devin, but I also knew how much of a pain in the ass college was. I rolled out of bed and went for a jog. That helped, but not like I wanted it to.

I sent Stu a text asking how things were going with him and the new girl he was seeing.

When my phone went off, I was excited to hear about someone else's life. Then I looked at who the message was from.

What was that all about last night?

Well, hello to you too, Shae.

Seriously. Brit. What was that?

If you're thinking I control my friends, you're horribly mistaken. I just throw the best damned parties you've ever been to.

Oh.

That was her last message to me for over a week.

Thirty-Two

JULIE FINALLY GAVE ME a date, and I planned like mad. I called Joe to make sure we could use his house. Then I called a local party planner to get me all the new trends. It may have been a congratulations party, but that didn't mean it couldn't be a party.

I considered also making it an engagement party, so I asked the planner if that would be tacky. She said no, especially if Julie and Cody planned to have Brian in the wedding. They did, so I told her to make it so. She emailed me designs, and I picked one out that was elegant yet simple. Pale blue and white. The party didn't have to match the wedding colors until the reception.

Of course, I held it at Osten's house. Catered, valet parking, the works. I pulled out all the shiny things for this; I'd been waiting so long. The gifts I'd hidden in the guest room closet came out and were wrapped. I was so excited to give them to Julie and Cody. Mere baubles, really. Swarovski crystal tree ornaments, a sterling silver picture frame I hoped the whole family would sit in. Trifles that would have meaning to Julie. Sentimental value was priceless, and I wanted them to know how much I appreciated their friendship. People think giving photo frames is dumb, but it's a psychological thing, I think.

The planner handled everything, coordinating with Osten's house staff and preferred vendors. It would be an exceptional affair. I arrived hours early to help direct things, but my planner had it all covered. I was able to relax some before the party.

I toured the house and grounds, admiring the decor. There were multiple gift tables set up—close to one hundred people would be there—half for engagement party gifts, the other half for gifts for Brian. I'd already loaded up almost a full table for the engagement party. For Brian's gifts, he and I had already discussed what he wanted from me. I was more than happy to oblige.

The party officially started at 1 p.m., though most people didn't show until just after. Julie, Cody, and Brian arrived around 12:30 and were greeted with drinks before I could even hug them. I understood why Joe kept the preferred vendor list he did.

Brian ran at me, book in hand, chattering on about how cool it was. It made my heart happy to know how much he loved the stories I'd given him. I hugged Julie and Cody, and they were a little more than upset with how extravagant the party was. I chose to keep my mouth shut about the band that would arrive by 1:30 and play a set for them.

I shooed them off to enjoy the decent weather outside so Brian and I could talk books and our trip to Universal. I also let him in on the surprise of who the band was. His squeal was all I needed.

"Mom is gonna freak! She LOVES them! Are you serious, Aunt Brit?"

"As a heart attack, kid. Don't ask me how I pulled this off. I don't know. All I did was make a phone call, and then it was all sorted out. I'll ask the lawyer I called later."

I hugged Brian and shooed him off, too. Then I went out-side to see the valet attendant.

"Hey there." I snuck up from behind Devin.

"Hey! Thanks for this gig, by the way. Now that the semes-ter's over, I can work more and not have to run out on your amazing eggs."

"Devin…"

"No, no. We discussed that. I was making a joke about the last night we were together is all."

"Okay. But really, my eggs aren't that great. I don't get why you all make such a fuss over them."

A blue Tesla sedan pulled up. Shae got out of the driver side. Devin greeted her and left to park her car. I, too, greeted her when she got closer.

"Look at you all fancy," I joked.

"You'd be surprised how not fancy I really am."

I looked at her, again trying to deduce what the hell was going on. Teslas weren't cheap. The charging system was also a few thousand dollars. I'd considered the Model X SUV, but the coolest thing about it had nothing to do with rocks or mud or anything I'd do with it.

"My apartment isn't that great; it's tiny. That's how I can afford the car if you were wondering"—she hugged me, still talking—"the fact that the place has charging systems blows my mind, but I'm not complaining. I get to look fancy and still be able to keep the lights on."

Well, that answered a bit of it, I supposed. I was curious, yeah, but it wasn't any of my business either. She volun-teered the information so easily, I had to wonder if it was an outright lie.

Devin came back and handed her a ticket. I told her I'd be right behind her and asked Devin for the tag number. He wasn't stupid. He knew damn well what I wanted it for. He wanted to know too. I called Stu and asked him to run the tag before he got here. He agreed and hung up.

I smiled at Devin and went to meet up with Shae.

The party was just getting started when the stage was being set up for the band. Apparently, it'd been made clear that they were a surprise for the happy family. All the gear was plain, no symbols or colors. Just black or white. The drum kit was also plain black and silver. I'd never seen the band play in person before, only videos, so I was a little disappointed. I shouldn't have been, but I was. Mixed feelings were running high today.

At 1:45, the band walked onto the stage in unassuming masks. Neither Julie nor Cody was paying any attention until Brian squeaked. They went to him, over by the stage, and realized. They looked around for me. I ducked and hid, laughing. Then the band started playing.

Fall Out Boy was a hit. Even for those who didn't like their music. Everyone was half-buzzed or plain-old happy. That's what made them all dance.

And then there were those of us who were fans, jumping around and dancing. We looked like fools mixed in with the group, and we didn't care. They played "Dance, Dance," "Sugar, We're Goin' Down," and so many others. They called Julie, Cody, and Brian up on stage, applauding and congratulating them. Then they called me, and I fought to not fangirl.

We got down from the stage, and the boys played one more song. My favorite. "I Don't Care." It was dedicated to me for being such a good friend. I almost cried but got too into the song.

They finished their set, congratulated the family again, and left. The four of us were high as stars in the sky. The adrenaline rush hadn't left yet. We hugged and cried and went inside for a breath of cooler air. It was a great afternoon.

The girls met us in the kitchen, all squeaking their surprise and gratitude for my phone call. Even Shae was enjoying herself. She was a self-professed metalhead. By now, I was positive that she was full of shit. I'd call her out on it as soon as Stu gave me the details. Knowing him as well as I did, he was probably running background on her too.

Thirty-Three

THE GROUP OF US threw back a shot—Brian had soda—and I went in search of the lawyer who gave this gift so freely. Turns out, the band was a client of his, and they were ecstatic to play when he asked. I didn't want to know why he'd bothered to mention it to the band, out of fear, that my professional life would quickly go to shit.

Stu arrived before 3:30 and pulled me aside.

"That Tesla is rented. But I have more to share about Shae."

For the next ten minutes, Stu went on about how Shae wasn't even her real name and that she was from Chicago. He also mentioned gangs and stalking, and that all had something to do with why she changed her name. I understood why she didn't tell anyone up front about it. It was a great way to scare off potential new friends. I felt bad that things had gotten so bad for her that she had to change her name and move. I had been able to take care of my stalkers, one way or another.

"That's why I'm so late."

"You're awesome, Stu. And what's her name?"

"We broke up. That's why you don't even know her name." He let out an uncomfortable laugh.

"I, uh, I…hope it's not because of me."

"No, it's me. I'm just not ready yet. No big deal."

I hugged him and pulled his arm. "Let's go grab drinks."

When everyone was together once more, we toasted to Julie, Cody, and Brian. And then it was time for speeches and cakes.

I gave mine first, talking about how much Julie had grown as a person and employee, about how we went to lunch one day and now there we were. Then Julie went, crying, and we couldn't understand most of what she said, but we knew. She was followed by Cody, who was followed by Brian. The crowd was given an opportunity to speak, and the girls went as a group. If this party was this emotional, the wedding would need two boxes of tissues per table, minimum.

By the time the final toast was given by our girlfriends, there wasn't a dry eye left. Including mine.

Shae came over to thank me for inviting her and to say bye. I wanted to confront her, but it wasn't the time. I could wait. Impatient or not, I had more digging to do. In my own database. I swore I knew her. That was what wasn't sitting right with me. My gut was screaming at me, calling her names like liar and twat. I needed to know why. And I would find out.

I let a week go by before texting Shae again. I asked her to meet for lunch, and she agreed. This time, we met at a pizza shop.

Shae bit off some of the slice in her hand and threw down half her cup of beer.

"Thanks for the invite. This place is great. I think it's the best pizza I've had in this city yet."

"No problem. I like it here. The pizza is perfectly greasy, and the atmosphere is happy," I said between bites.

We talked and caught up with each other. She had no clue that I knew things about her. I'd found out she'd temped for me under her previous name, which made me wonder a lot of different things.

"Can I ask you something personal?"

She swallowed and gave me a hard look. No words came out of her mouth, nor did she move her head in a way that said yes or no. She took another bite, continuing to study me.

I kept eating. This was now awkward as fuck, and I had put us there.

"Yes."

Well, thanks.

"What happened that you left here and moved to Chicago and now you're back?"

"Stupid. Ass. Boyfriend. That's what happened." She finished her beer and stood to get another. I offered to grab it for her, but she insisted.

While she was gone, I thought about what she said. We do crazy things for those we love. I was just as guilty of that. I decided to stop questioning and let her come around. Now that she told me the start, she'd eventually tell me the rest.

Shae came back, handing me a beer too.

"I figured you could use another. Anyway, where was I? Oh, right. So I followed my ex up there. I was in love and stupid. Long story, but he was a gang member, and I never knew until he brought one of his crew home, and that guy started calling me a lot and basically stalking me. Then it got worse. I saw some shit. I take it you remember me?"

"Sort of. I also had you checked out. Yes. I screen everyone in my life." I laughed. "You never know when you've befriended a psycho." I ignored her insinuation that *she* remembered *me*.

We toasted to old lives gone and new friends. On our walk to the parking garage, Shae was grateful I had asked. She said she felt a weight lifted.

We hugged bye and went our separate ways. I couldn't help but think about what Shae's last words were on the subject.

"I feel so much better. Like a weight lifted from my chest."

That wouldn't be all she'd feel.

Acknowledgments

This book, let alone series, wouldn't be possible without the following people and references:

Practical Homicide Investigation (5th Edition) by way of a Thomas Harris acknowledgement. The FBI's *Serial Murder Multi-Disciplinary Perspectives for Investigators* Report (available free online), and *psychologytoday.com* for helping me add the necessary depth to Britney.

Ret. Sgt. Chuck Burns for his consultation where the textbook didn't answer specific questions.

Justin D., for helping me on ridiculously short notice with some nicknames.

Nathan, for his advice and invitations. I'm so very grateful I finally decided to take you up.

Mark…sweet Mark. Without you, I wouldn't be here. I love you more than I can express and always will.

Jason, for the awesome editing and blurbs and feedback and advice and just being you. You have made me the writer I am today. Let's not get arrested, please. At least not before we make that money.

Also by
Amanda Byrd

13 Reasons for Murder:

Politeness Kills (#1)

Meathead (#2)

Philistines (#3)

Hungry (#4)

Bad Blood (#5)

Betrayal (#6)

Disillusioned (#7)
Harlot (#8) *2023*

The Morgan Davis Serials

The Girl at the Bottom of the Ocean (#1)

Before You Die (#2)

Serial Women of History
Amelia Earhart, Serial Killer *2023*

Anthologies

Thrill of the Hunt: Cabin Fever (Thrill of the Hunt Anthology Book 6)